I0607544

My Head is Missing

Also available from Evertype:
Kwaidan: Stories and Studies of Strange Things
Lafcadio Hearn, illustrated by Mathew Staunton

Éist leis an gCruinne (2014)
Gabriel Rosenstock

The Partisan and other stories (2014)
Gabriel Rosenstock, illustrated by Mathew Staunton

The Naked Octopus (2013)
Gabriel Rosenstock & Mariko Sumikura, illustrated by Mathew Staunton

Fluttering their way into my head: an exploration of Haiku for young people
(2014)
Gabriel Rosenstock, illustrated by Mathew Staunton

I Met a Man from Artikelly: Verse for the young and young at heart (2014)
Gabriel Rosenstock, illustrated by Mathew Staunton

Available from our friends at The Onslaught Press:
behind the yew hedge (2015)
Gabriel Rosenstock & Mathew Staunton

Antlered Stag of Dawn (2015)
Gabriel Rosenstock, John McDonald, & Mariko Sumikura

Judgement Day (2016)
Gabriel Rosenstock & Karl Waldmann

My Head is Missing

A Kerry Detective Story

Gabriel Rosenstock

evertype

2016

Published by Evertype, 73 Woodgrove, Portlaoise, R32 ENP6, Ireland. *www.evertype.com*.

This edition © 2016 Michael Everson.
Text © 2012–2016 Gabriel Rosenstock. First published electronically in 2012 by Original Writing, Dublin.

All rights reserved. No part of this publication may be reproduced, stored in a retrieval system, or transmitted, in any form or by any means, electronic, mechanical, photocopying, recording, or otherwise, without the prior permission in writing of the Publisher, or as expressly permitted by law, or under terms agreed with the appropriate reprographics rights organization.

A catalogue record for this book is available from the British Library.

ISBN-10 1-78201-181-1
ISBN-13 978-1-78201-181-1

Typeset in Dutch Medieval Pro, Baskerville, **Transport**, and Atsinvsda by Michael Everson.

Cover design by Mathew Staunton.

Printed and bound by LightningSource.

Contents

For Mícheál Ó hAodha

My Head is Missing

My mind is an unknown insect, searching for its name.

—Dutch Diaries (destroyed) of Shane O'Neil

Chapter 1

A wee kitten

May Kelly sailed unannounced into the freshly painted office of the KDA (Kerry Detective Agency) and extended a hefty paw, indicating that she was going to shake the detective's hand. Quite vigorously at that. Whether he liked it or not. He did, he thought, at least the first few seconds of the flesh-pressing.

"Welcome," says she, "welcome to Powl Duv. Welcome back, I suppose I should say." Her voice was too vehement for the room, much too thunderous for today's lifestyle, a voice suited to hollering from one field to another, or calling men in from turf-cutting for a pot of steaming, strong tea. Long ago. Something like that, Shane surmised. Not that he had ever seen turf being cut or had ever in his fifty-odd years on this planet sipped tea, or anything else, in the middle of a bog. No, not that he could remember.

Shane O'Neil blinked. He had been wondering what it might be like, a welcome from one or two of the locals. What a powerful grip she had. His little finger seemed to be glued to the one next to it! In all his years abroad he never experienced such a grip. At least, not from a friendly source. And definitely not from a female. Now, back in his mother's ancestral home, he was getting first-hand evidence of the mettle you could expect from the women of Powl Duv. Strong women. Ancient stock. Pre-Celtic some of them. How many of these types were about?

His mother's home. He didn't want to call it his own. Not yet. He had too few memories of it. But maybe they would come back, prompted by a sound, a taste, a colour, a scent. Or return unprompted, a word or two appearing on a Scrabble board.

"Take a seat," said Shane, offering her his own new office chair, quickly calculating that it was the one best suited to her girth. First time for everything and a first time for a first client to take a seat in his sturdy new chair. Was she a client or just a neighbour introducing herself? He had gone over such phrases as "Take a seat" many times in his mind. Where had all those phrases gone?

"That I will," says May Kelly, grimacing as she suppressed a slight groan and sat down, holding her left hip. It was a tight enough fit. "It's on my feet I am since the neighbour's cock started shoutin like it was the end of the world and it still pitch black all over Kerry. Glory be to God! There must be a law agin it, is there? There was a time when a cock knew when to crow and when to shut up." Shane thought about this for a moment. Law-breaking roosters. Unfamiliar territory. Did everybody around here speak like May Kelly?

"And then the fridge died on me, so it did. Sang its last sad little song. Ould age, I suspect. Arthritis or somethin. Goin the same way meself, I am. Any cure for a stiff hip? Cod liver oil, they say. It's not workin on me. Maybe it's all a cod. What do you think?"

Shane shrugged. He wasn't accustomed to being asked for advice, not from women with dodgy hips. Not from anybody. Don't ask me any intimate questions please. The last thing I am is a gynaecologist.

She suddenly produced a plastic bottle which from its label Shane deduced had once held red lemonade.

"Here, asthore, have some buttermilk. I'm afraid it might go off on me." As in run off? Disappear? Go sour, of course, thought Shane. Concentrate, man. She fixed an unsteady gaze on him, curious as to what his reaction might be to that token gift of hers. Would he be embarrassed? If so, she might not be able to trust him. She was already mistrustful of his swivel chair.

Buttermilk? What am I to do with this? Bake bread? Drink it down like a man? She moved around in the chair and swivelled a bit. That chair is going to have to go. He needed a chair to suit all clients, all

6

girths. Why hadn't he spent a little longer studying the catalogue? That's what comes from working far too long in an office where all such decisions are made for you. Furniture. Heating. Lighting.

He put the buttermilk safely aside. May Kelly adjusted herself more comfortably in the chair and leaned back a little as though about to launch into outer space. She herself could have come from there. You're no slave to fashion, are you? Knit that cardigan yourself during the long wintry nights of Powl Duv? You are a throwback to another era, are you not? A lost time? If so, I'm in the right place. The 21st century is still fairly new but I've already seen enough of it. Lost time is what I'm looking for. Lost years.

"Haven't had buttermilk since Noah was in short trousers. Can I offer you anything, Miss—?"

"May!"

"Of course, Miss May. I stand corrected. May I offer you—?"

"May's the name. B & B's me game. May Kelly."

Shane looked at her for a moment and nodded.

"A drop of tea, perhaps?"

"I've had me tay, thank you. Buckets of it, thank you, Mr O'Neil. Not meanin to be impertinent or anythin but I'm the only one that makes tay the way I like it. I'd say your brew wouldn't be strong enough for me, do you know the way? When I makes tay I makes tay and when I makes water I makes water. Did ye ever hear that? 'Tis a sayin we had around here. That is, when we had people, a population. Anyway, I've come today about Bella."

Tay! I was in short pants when last I heard it said that way. Why is she looking at me like that? Oh, yes. Bella!

Shane O'Neil's brain went into top gear. A daughter gone missing, perhaps. Run off somewhere. Pursuing some undesirable member of the male species? Well, this is the type of thing that had brought him to Kerry after all. Early retirement from international policing. Why not do some part-time detection? As a hobby, of course. At his own pace. Refurbish his mother's old home; convert the ground floor into an office. Sleep upstairs. The sleep of the just? The dream was now becoming a reality. Of sorts. The smell of fresh paint to prove it. Now that he noticed it, May exuded a faint odour, one which competed not too subtly with the paint. What was it? Buttermilk?

"Bella? Tell me more."

"You've done a nice job here so you have."

"Not bad," Shane admitted, attempting a smile. "I got a bit of help, of course."

"There isn't a—?" She looked around again.

What are you looking for? A toilet?

"No, I can see there isn't," she said.

"What?" asked Shane, his powers of detection not firing on all cylinders yet.

"A Mrs O'Neil? No, she'd have flowers, wouldn't she? Bluebells, I expect, they'd go nice now with them colours. Do you like bluebells?"

"Haven't much experience of bluebells. Tulips. Holland, where I've been living, mostly, up to now, loads of tulips. Enough for every household in Kerry."

"Don't like the tulip. Has a bit of an opinion of itself."

No idea what you mean by that.

She looked around, cautiously, not accustomed to the swivel chair, but clearly enjoying the sensation nonetheless. Her powers of detection were probably more advanced than his, he mused, allowing himself another little smile. It felt more like a curling of the lip than a smile.

"Well, Mr O'Neil, she's only this size, if she's that."

May Kelly's gesture suggested to Shane that Bella was too small to be running away from home or chasing undesirable males. In fact, Bella was too small to be human.

"Are we talking about a dog here, May?"

The woman raised an index finger and wagged it at him. Her teeth were horrific.

"Oh, it's yerself is the smart one, all right. I can see you've the makings of a grand defective. A cat. A cat is what she is. White. With one black ear. But you were close. I'll grant you that." She laughed. She wasn't going to win many prizes for those teeth.

Hold on. Defective? Did she say "defective"? God, say not. My first case. A missing cat. Couldn't be true. Say it's not true. What would the boys in Europol have to say about all this? Maybe she's right. He smiled, wanly. Maybe I am what she says—a defective.

"Kitten, really," said May as though reading his thoughts.

Perhaps he should have put up a sign. We don't find missing pets. He was loath to put up any sign, other than KDA in mock-Celtic lettering. The way one or two passers by stared at it, he knew he was going to have to replace that sign at once. Who were those people? Locals? Visitors? Probably right about the sign, whoever they were. He should be as conventional as possible. Let's wait, he admonished himself, wait and see. Get to know the sensitivities and prejudices of the locals. Don't attract too much attention to yourself. Easy does it.

"There's not many that come back to the ould sod after havin been away for so long." She studied him, as if wondering if it really was Shane O'Neil returned. "There was a man from these parts and hadn't he booked himself into my B & B and all and didn't I even go to the bus meself to welcome him back, so I did. Must be five years ago if it's a day. Wouldn't get off the bus, poor divil. Couldn't. Looked at me with big watery eyes like a seal below in Dingle, so he did, and the bus driver shoutin at him and all. Get off, says he, you're here. Powl Duv. No. Wouldn't budge. Stuck to the seat, he was. Terrible. Couldn't do it. Couldn't come home again. Couldn't breathe the sweet air of Powl Duv again. A Moriarty, he was. A brand new cap on his head and all. What good was it? He had a sister a nun out in Maryland. Medical Missionaries of Mary. All the family scattered to the four winds. Too long in Huddersfield he was, poor man. Among all them Connemara people and English folk and Patrickstanis and all the rest of em. Can you imagine it?"

"Have you a photo?"

"Of Moriarty?"

"Bella."

"Bella? A photo?"

May Kelly laughed and swivelled in the chair.

"Photo! That I have not. No no. There's a photo of the Sacred Heart hanging above the range but that's about it. Sure I don't even have a photo of me own husband. And why would I and he after lavin me, the *leábharaic*."

(If that last word described the gentleman who had upped and gone, Shane was none the wiser.) What am I to do? Sympathize? Offer to track him down? When had the aforementioned gentleman made his exodus?

"I'd a photo once of the Little Flower that a priest gave me. He was a Capuchin. You know, with a beard. Like Padre Pio. I gave it away. You know who I'm talkin about, don't you?" Shane nodded. She felt reassured that she wasn't talking to a pagan.

"Little Flower. St Therese of Liseux. Oh, I don't know..." She sighed. "You can't be prayin to saintly nuns to bring you good luck and happiness and all that, especially if they weren't all that happy themselves. In their own lives. Would you agree? What did the poet say, the one that's buried yonder in Dureen. Life is a dream, he said, a dream inside in a dream. He said that, so he did. Everyone around here knows it. When you wake up from the dream—if you ever do, that is— you're still in a dream, he said. Or somethin like that. What did he mean by all that? Quare ould talk if you ask me. Where were we?"

She looked into Shane's eyes as if they held the answer to a riddle or something. Where were we indeed? Shane had no idea. St Therese. And—was there some mention of a poet? Where were all those stock phrases that he had practiced? *Take a seat* was the only one that came to mind right then. And she was already well settled in her seat. Come on, man, think! This was pathetic!

"It's dreamin I am... Photos? Photos, yes, that was it. No, no time for em. Fella tried to sell me a photo of the house once. Aerial view, says he, taken by a satellite, says he. Did ye ever hear such carry on! Where would the likes of that mangy, stray dog get a satellite! If I want an aerial view of my house, I'll become a witch, says I, and examine it rightly in my own time and on my own broom and from up above. An aerial view! And if that's really what it was, I don't remember anyone askin me for permission. Is there a law agin it? I was goin to write a letter to the *Kerryman* about it. But what's the point? I don't see the *Kerryman* puttin a stop to them sputniks and satellites, do you?" She snorted contemptuously.

Sputnik? Haven't heard that word since I was a child. Some words were slow to disappear in Powl Duv. Shane picked up a biro and doodled on his new note pad. He wrote the word SPUTNIK in big letters. We were all looking up and we didn't know what to expect and it was only like the glow of a cigarette in the dark. Nothing special at all. Was my father there, looking up at the sky. "There it is!" Was that my father's voice? Is that all of him that's left?

"Haven't done pets before..." No, nor humans either if the truth be known.

"No matter. I've a power of faith in you!" exclaimed May. "And anyway, you're the only defective within a dunkey's roar of Powl Duv. There was a fella in Tralee once, all right, but he didn't last long. God, no. What was his name?"

"No idea."

Shane regretted opening his mouth. It wasn't a question. Of course not. Most questions in Powl Duv were rhetorical questions. You rarely asked a real question. He'd love to have a mint there and then, something to focus on, to relieve the tension.

May Kelly frowned. It made her look older.

"Didn't last long at all at all. How could he? No connection to the place whatsoever. And he used the Irish version of his name. No one could spell it. Down from Dublin. No connection in the wide world to Kerry. What was he hidin at all that he used the Irish version of his name? I heard of someone who started talkin to him in Irish and couldn't get an answer out of him. Hadn't a word of it. Was he from Dublin at all? He could have been a Romanian, pretendin to be Irish. There was somethin about him. Somethin foreign, like. Not like yerself and your mother, and all her people, all from here and her mother agin before her. God be good to them all. Used to scratch his head a lot, that fella in Tralee, pretendin to be figurin things out. Sure people saw through him, they were only laughin at him and the poor man, didn't the drink take an awful howlt of him after a while, a fierce howlt I can tell you; swung him around and around, so it did, swung him around so fasht he didn't know easht from wesht and the thin bit of a wisp of hair coverin his bald patch at the mercy of all the Kerry winds. Part of his problem, poor man, was that he couldn't get his tongue around the local names. He had some kind of an impediment when it came to names. Skrahancockgower for instance. Not a hope, man! You'd think it was the Latin or the Greek he was talkin when he came out with the names. How could you put any business in the way of a man who couldn't pronounce Skrahancockgower, for God's sake?"

"Good point. Skrahan—?"

"Cockgower. It's only down the road, a mile or two."

"Of course."

Where does one go from here?

"May I get a description of Bella from you?" asked Shane, tearing out a page that was covered with incoherent doodles. He crumpled the sheet and threw it absentmindedly into the fireplace. While taking notes he began to make small talk and casually established a token fee for his services. A good first step. It wouldn't do for May Kelly to say he was an extortionist. Might he have undercharged her? Too late. He tried to pronounce Skrahancockgower, silently, to himself. He had a fairly good ear. Picked up Dutch quite well. That's all you had to do. Listen, listen, listen. Break up the words into little pieces, don't be afraid of them. Skrahan-cock-gower. Put all the pieces back together again. Recite the name, like a nursery rhyme. Best way to remember. He'd had to do that in Holland. It worked.

"I'll be talkin to you." She extricated herself clumsily from the swivel chair, clearly unfamiliar with the dynamics involved.

"God, I nearly took off there! That would be one for the *Kerryman*, wouldn't it? 'Kerry Woman in Orbit'. I must get one of these. What are they called?"

"Swivel chairs, I think." Shouldn't say "I think". Be positive. Authoritative.

12

"My first time swivellin. Are they expensive? Would I get one at an auction, do you think?"

That strong grip again. The way he was handled in the orphanage? No. The way he might shove a criminal into a car? No. What criminals? Desk-bound all his life. May's grip was something he hadn't known. Not for years. This was a different energy altogether. A caring strength, a reassuring strength. Did she know how strong she was? Shane rubbed his hands together to get the circulation back into them.

He watched her disappear down the short gravel path and as she did so she cast a disapproving eye on the flowerless verges. Or was it a more pitying eye? May Kelly. His first client. Fifty euros now. Another fifty later. For Bella—alive, of course. Had he arrived ten years earlier he could have charged what he liked. The country was awash with money. But their horns had been pulled in of late. Migrants—those lucky ones who had saved their money—were slowly drifting back to Eastern Europe, to Romania, Bulgaria, Latvia, and Poland.

May Kelly. A strong, big-boned lump of a woman, slightly shabby in her faded jeans. A woman with the hands of a hammer thrower. He watched her fade into the brightening air. Was that a phrase from a song? Or a poem? Anyway, what was he supposed to do about Bella? "Right!" he said aloud, almost startling himself. One thing was certain, he wasn't going to find her dozing quietly in some corner of his office. Best to get out again. Breathe the air. Get a proper feel for the village. The people.

A bilingual sign outside the village proclaimed

Poll Dubh
POWL DUV
Daonra – Population 36

Someone had drawn a line through the figure 35. It was now 36. Was the number 36? Officially? If so, where was the rest of the population? They hadn't all moved to a holiday home in France or Spain, had they? Shane had thought of chasing the sun as well, at one point. But

13

something else whispered to him and whatever it was had called him back to Powl Duv, to where he first saw the light of day, where he first tasted his mother's milk on his lips, a place that existed before the world darkened for him. Before he was taken away.

He looked out the window, as if searching for a clue, a clue to all of it. A crow glided silently by. On its way to Dureen Wood. The wind buffeted it a few times but the crow flapped its wings, determined to reach Dureen.

What could he remember of his childhood here? He wasn't sure. Kaleidoscopic images and sounds, occasional flashes every so often, pieces of a jigsaw that never quite came together. Smells. Sour odours. The colours of the past had their own smells. Yellow was milky. Red was acrid. And music, especially Irish music: brown and earthy, smelling of clay. Or green. Or silvery. Sometimes, depending on the tune, he could feel the mountain air in his nostrils again, the tingle and taste of the stream-water on his tongue. Then the music would have a purple feel. Sometimes golden. Was it all in the mind? It didn't make much sense. Once he had tried to imitate the dawn chorus on the tin whistle. He gave up, however: it was a task which needed more than one lifespan, more musical skills than he possessed.

Memories? They were few and far between. Do we need them? Maybe they would come when needed. At times he felt that the Kerry Detective Agency was not what he wanted himself at all. He just needed to find himself, didn't he? Nothing or nobody else just himself alone. Himself. Or his "self"? Or a memory of who he had once been, some scintilla of his lost childhood. A rhyme. An incomplete phrase. A loving hand tussling his hair. Whose? When? Fragments. Figments of imagination. Fig—ments? A fig. He had eaten a fig once. Hadn't he? But when? Where? Who had given it to him? Darkness swirling. The fig. Its colour. Texture. Taste. Shape. Size. Seeds. Why remember a fig and not your father's face? Ah, why try to remember any more? Live in the present, he told himself. The now. He wasn't even sure what the "now" was anymore, or if there even was a "now".

14

He glanced in the mirror. He could pass for fifty. Easily. Standing to attention in front of the mirror he began to practise what he considered his serious smile. A smile that showed him as friendly. It had a serious side to it, this smile of his, depending which eye you looked into. Somehow Shane had the knack of attracting people to that serious eye. If he thought they needed him to appear... well, serious. Serious, without being ghoulish. One eye you get from your father, the other from your mother. That's why both eyes are different, never the same. Or so he had read, somewhere. Now, which eye did he get from his mother? The left or the right?

He decided to spend the rest of the day pottering about, checking various appliances, making sure that everything worked; after all, he had ploughed his life savings into this project. Now and again he glanced at the phone, wondering would it ring. He checked taps, drains, windows, doors. Checked the shed and its supply of turf. They'll soon make it illegal, the supplier had told him. Enjoy it while you can. Mark my words, he said. Someone in Europe will say stop burning turf. Where will we all be then?

Holland seemed very far away now. The European landmass was another world. Ireland is an island, he reminded himself, with an insular mentality to go with it. And Ireland herself has hundreds of islands. Maybe Powl Duv is just a first stop, he thought. Why not go further? To one of the islands. The smell of the turf caused his mind to drift, like smoke. It was one of the few certain memories he still had from childhood, the smell of turf. Unmistakeable. His former colleagues looked at him with some amusement when he confessed that turf was one of the things that drew him back to Ireland. Not that he had shared much with that lot. No one knew his dreams, his desires. No one on this earth.

Look! He had lit his first fire. He pulled a chair up and sat in front of it, in respectful silence. Adding another sod to the fire, he saw that this was a nightly ritual he could easily endure. Whatever else his erstwhile colleagues may or may not have, they haven't these tongues of flame, this aroma. It is something that lives and moves. And it is I—I that have

15

brought it to life, something that was asleep for thousands and thousands of years. Something that was once a tree, that grew on its own and fell one day unseen, unheard, slowly over millennia becoming one with the bog.

Fireplace, the cradle of civilization. Civilization was unimaginable without an open fire. Without fire, man would have lost touch with himself, with others. For millennia it had been the centre of the home, where food was cooked, water boiled, limbs warmed. Around which stories were told, long into the night. And now, at last, he had a fire of his own. A living link to the past. Not only to his mother's time. Back, back, back to hunter-gatherer man when fire was warmth and survival, when wild fire was first tamed by man, those dancing flames that kept bears and wolves away. He looked at the flaming turf. The fire was alive and he too had come alive, truly alive for the first time in a wearisome stretch of years. A frost within him was beginning to thaw. Slowly. Surely.

He would settle in here with the help and comfort of the fire, if nothing else. Soon the house would get to know him. Floors would know his footfall, chairs his shape, the bed his dreams, his nightmares. The mirror his quest. Trees, walls will get to know him, will refract his thoughts, voiced and unvoiced. The very air itself will bless him and protect him. How different is the air here, the water, the light. Light that enters Dureen Wood is not the same light that emerges. It is thinner, more liquid, greener when it comes out. It has changed. He too would change.

He will become a familiar, friendly figure. And none need fear him. Not any more. Of course, none ever did—but imagining that they did helped one to get through the day with its growing mountain of paperwork, a mountain once levelled that sprang up again, year in, year out; nothing relieved this weight except those people from the underworld. They quaked at the very sight of me, at the sound of my name, Shane O'Neil, scourge of the underworld.

That was how he had survived. And now, in Powl Duv, he was determined to hold his head high, higher than he ever had before. His ancestors had left Ireland at the beginning of the seventeenth century.

16

Wild Geese. At the beginning of the twenty first century, here he was now returning home. What did it all mean, this coming and going?

What had he felt when he visited the church of San Pietro, Montorio, Rome, many years ago and gazed at those haunting words:

D.O.M
Hugonis Principis ONelli
OSSA

To God the best and the greatest
Hugh Prince O'Neill
BONES

What had he felt? Reverence? Sadness? Awe? Would those bones cry out if they knew that a descendant of the Great Ó Néill was being paid now to search for a missing feline?

He listened to the silence. It was silence that had called him here, the promise of silence, stillness. It washed over him. Not in waves but in oceans. Is this what it feels like, to be at peace?

That night he dreamed of forests and forest floors of pine needles. Each one a clue. To what?

From the PRIVATE DIARY of Shane O'Neill

Settling in OK. Well, no. Not really. Not fully. Not yet. Well... reasonably well. Maybe. Must give myself more time. The rest of my life ahead of me. This is Powl Duv, not The Hague. Relax. There are no more reports to be read.

It's hard to believe. Somebody else is ploughing through all those reports now and writing more reports about reports. Don't say you miss it. You don't. You can't. You won't. How could you miss something like that? Unless prisoners miss their jailors. Some of them do. Don't say— never ever let me hear you say that you miss Raamweg 47. It's slowly dissolving in your mind, Raamweg 47. Isn't it? Like a dream. You will forget it. When it comes down to it, a dream that lasted years is the same as a dream that lasts a night, or a few minutes, or a few seconds. Reports. They could knock down every tree in Dureen Wood and still not have enough paper for those reports. And summaries of reports because no one has any time to read full reports anymore. Bullet points. He specialized in bullet points. It was an art in itself.

❖

Do they know, really? Do they half-suspect that I'm not a detective? They haven't had time to figure me out yet, have they? Shane O'Neil. Pen-pusher extraordinaire. One of Europe's finest. If only they knew the real story. Day after day. Week after week. Month after month. Year after year. Reports. Piling up, like toxic waste.

❖

May Kelly's hand in mine. I can't remember when a woman's hand was last in mine. I wouldn't want to arm-wrestle with her. Not likely.

❖

Hello, robin! You've seen more action in your short life than I have, haven't you? Hopping from branch to branch. From tree to tree. How would you like to be sitting behind a desk for thirty years, robin, first with Interpol, then with Europol? Insane, isn't it? Of course it is. Totally insane. Why did I do it? What else was there to do? I could have walked away. Yes, I could. And I did in the end. Left it late, though, didn't I? Yes. Don't go away, robin. Stay. Tell me who you are. What you are. Tell me a secret. Tell me who I am. What I am. What am I, go on robin! Tell me about Powl Duv. Go on! Tell me all about it. I'm sure you know some secrets. I'd say you peep into lots of windows. Who killed Cock Robin? I, said the Sparrow, with my bow and arrow. I killed Cock Robin. Now, where did that come from just now? Is it a poem or a play? Or something else? Something I learned as a child? I'm hearing things, little robin. There were no poems in the orphanage, as far as I can remember. Are you helping me to remember things? Little children never give pain to things that feel and live. Let the gentle robin come, for the crumb you save at home. Now where did that one come from? Another poem? Are there any other robin poems buried in my memory? Don't go away, robin. I remember you. I know you. Or one of your ancestors anyhow. Your great great grandfather, or something. He probably sat on that very branch. That's possible. Isn't it? Of course. I might have known him. Spoken to him. Just as I'm speaking to you now. Isn't that a strange one? You know I'm talking to you, don't you? There's something telepathic in the air of Powl Duv, isn't there? How trustingly you look in at me. My boss—the Sphinx—she never looked at me like that. Not from the very first day. Not since the interview for the job, not then nor since. The way that you look at me now, the way I look at you, with such honesty and clarity. Don't go!

❖

Powl Duv. Funny name, that. They tell me that it means "black hole". Who would want to call a place by such a name? Do I really want to be here? OK, it's just one big lie from start to finish. Sure. Kerry Detective Agency. Big fat lie. I know it. But can I keep it up, I wonder. Well, why not? I don't see why not. It's not such a big lie, is it? It's only a fib. The licence looks genuine enough. Who's going to question it? I'm not harming anyone. Not deliberately. Might even do some good? Who knows? We'll give it a whirl anyway. It can't be worse than thirty years behind a desk. What good did that do? No good at all. Had to stand in front of a mirror every evening when I got home and push my shoulders back. If I didn't do that I'd have a stoop.

He's gone. The robin. His little red breast and his curious eye. Everything's just coming and going, going and coming all the time. Non-stop. I'd have liked to have talked to that robin a bit more. That's something I can do here. I really can feel it. I can commune with nature here. I can talk to stones and grass and ivy about my pen-pushing days. And when the pen retired, it was the computer. I tell the stones all this and they look at me with their grey faces. More work they created, those computers. Not less. I declare this to the trees and they quiver. I'd have liked to have talked more to that robin. Tell him everything. Somebody did something to my computer, robin. I know it. Yes indeed. Slowed it down. Somebody got into the computer. Why? Because someone wanted something. What? Promotion. Of course. No, I can't prove it. But it makes sense. It wasn't going slower every day of its own accord, was it? O'Neil is falling behind a bit, isn't he? Me? No, I wasn't. Damn well sure I wasn't. Somebody had slowed the computer down. They know how to do that. They're doing it all the time. And I was getting this stuff coming up on my screen that I couldn't erase. And how come the supervisor arrives just as I am trying to get rid of that crap? What is that stuff, she said, her lip curling, baring her fangs. I don't know, I said, I've been trying to get rid of it all morning. And she just looked at me. Pityingly. Or did she know something? Was she in on it too? Wouldn't surprise me.

❖

Powl Duv. I'm not really here, am I? It appears I am. In Kerry. Ireland. It has happened. I'm here. I sometimes don't know how I got here. I was in a bit of a daze. Now that I'm looking around me properly, I can see that there are far worse places on the planet. What is it I hoped to find here? And end to all the coming and going. The traffic. The trafficking. Bullet points.

Bella! I'd have laughed but I've forgotten how to laugh. Almost. How am I going to learn how to laugh again? I used to know how to laugh. Now I don't know if I'd recognize the sound of my own laughter. If I ever laugh again, will it be a new kind of laughter? Will it have a new ring to it? Will it be shorter, or longer, or louder or softer or—I think I need to get out more often. Out into the air. Good country air. I need to breathe. Maybe I haven't enough air in my lungs to be able to laugh. Maybe that's it. That could be it. It could be as simple as that.

I wanted the robin to explain something to me, didn't I? But what? Explain what? Is that a sane question to ask? Why am I always questioning everything, everybody, including myself? Let things be. Just let them be. People. And places. Robins. Questions. Just let them happen. Don't dig too deep. Or you'll fall into a hole. Don't question. Don't destroy everything again.

❖

The robin's gone. Gone. Gone into a void. With all its rosy robiness. How boldly it looked at me for a second. Just a split second. Gone. Where's he gone, Mr Detective? What exactly went through its little brain to say, I'm out of here, this guy is just looking out the window sheepishly, nothing of interest here.

Hold on, I can pull this off. Steady. Easy, now. Easy. Don't panic. Easy does it.

A herd of goats producing Organic Kerry Goat's Cheese. Now, that I couldn't manage. No. So, easy does it, easy, Shane. That's it. Nice. And. Easy. KDA. This you can pull off. With a bit of luck. Patience. Discretion. Write down the words, keep them coming, these thoughts, here, in your diary, just as they come to you. And keep it safe. Keep it secret.

KDA, keep saying it and you'll believe it. So will others. KDA. Kerry Detective Agency. It's good. Very good. KDA, that's you. Keep saying it. It's got to be as familiar as bread, as rain. KDA. What's wrong with it? Nothing wrong with it. KDA. Has a ring to it. Like IRA. Well, not exactly. KDA. Not everyone is going to approve. So? So what if you have critics. Enemies. So what? More the better. You've never really had any serious challenge in all your life, have you? Now's your chance. Start drinking buttermilk—or whatever it takes to be... what? Normal. A Powl Duv man. Integrate.

❖

Mammy... was it Mammy I called you, or Mamma? Mum? You wanted me to come back to this house, didn't you? The builder from Tralee and his Polish crew, when we walked about this house and talked about what we could and couldn't do, within the budget, walking every inch of this crumbling house, I picked up a broken comb. A white comb, with missing teeth. Was it yours, Mammy? Did you comb your hair with it fifty odd years ago? Or mine? Did you comb my hair with it? I look at things. I look at things that are not there as well. I listen. I'm trying to listen. Trying to make sense. There is no sense. I know that. But I'm trying to find some pattern, a few clues. I may not be a detective, in the strict sense. But I need to be. I have to be. I must get to the bottom of things. A lot of things. I have to. I've let too much slip by. Too many years. Too many moments with nothing happening. No sunshine. No rain. No air. Just words. Words on paper. The paper mounting. And what have I got? Friends? None. A pension. And as we say bye-bye to Shane O'Neil... he had to read it. He didn't know who the hell I was. Where I'd come from. What I had contributed to the organization. I was just some kind of dry rot they were getting rid of. The office would be fresher once I had gone. And we thank Shane for—for what? For not

22

setting fire to the building? I had thought of it. More than once. That would be something for Europol to solve.

Raamweg 47, The Hague. It had magic, at first. Novelty. But over the years, whenever I heard the address or saw it written down, I tasted something vinegary in the back of my throat. Will Powl Duv turn out to be like that? Like Raamweg 47? Look at it. The syllables spell pure horror now. At least, I'm my own boss here. No hackers here because there's no computer. Bliss!

❖

Finally took down the KDA sign. Don't need it. It was ostentatious. Pretentious. Loath to dump it, though. Might keep it in the attic.

❖

I'll come back to you, Diary. Tired now. Sleepy. Good night. Must find a safe place for you, tuck you in snugly for the night.

I long to speak in the language of molluscs.

—Dutch Diaries (destroyed) of Shane O'Neil

Chapter 2

A Poet and his Charms

Next day, his mind went over the few, paltry details that May Kelly had given him. Had he enough to go on? Not really. He would have to ring her. Or simply call in? She wasn't a world away. Certain matters were in need of clarification. What had he done with her card? Was it in his wallet? No. It was in his pocket, the last pocket he searched.

> COOLEEN
> Bed and Breakfast
> Main Street
> Powl Duv (twenty minutes at most from Tralee)
> Co. Kerry
> Proprietor: May Kelly (widow)

Main Street. He liked that. Powl Duv had only one street, as far as he could detect. Widow? What a strange thing to have on a card. Was she fishing for a husband? He dialled.

"Cooleen, B & B. Céad míle fáilte, a hundred thousand welcomes. Rooms available. May here. Hello?" She was slightly breathless.

"Shane here, May, Shane O'Neil."

"Who? Oh, it's only yerself. I'm just in the door, Shane. You haven't found her already, have you?"

"No no. Just... a few things I didn't ask you, May. I can call you May?"

"You can call me anythin so long as you don't call me too early in the mornin! Sure haven't I the neighbour's cock to do that for me, may it meet a sudden end before long."

"Indeed." He felt in need of a mint. Rummaging in his pocket he found none.

"Might I ask, did you put a notice up anywhere?"

"Notice? What kind of notice?"

" You know. Notice! About Bella. Being missing?"

"God, no I didn't, Mr O'Neil. And I won't either. I wouldn't like to be attractin too much attention to meself, don't you know?"

"Oh, really?"

"Better keep it nice and quiet between ourselves. Sure you don't want the whole world to be knowin your business. Between yerself and meself. Sure look, if you put up a notice you could be attractin all sorts of unsavoury types. Do you know what I mean?"

"Not exactly," said Shane. What did she mean?

"Ransom notes. Stuff like that. Sure, Tralee is gettin as bad as Miami!" Is she nuts?

"Is it? Oh! Well, fair enough. We'll keep it... nice and quiet then, as you say, May. Right so. Good. Bye, May."

"Bye-bye. And—Mr O'Neil?"

"Shane!"

"Good luck!"

He went outside, leaving the door open behind him, and looked around. The sky was much bluer today than he had ever seen it abroad. It appeared to extend further than his accustomed field of vision. Two magpies were chatting on a stone wall. Suddenly he felt a little despondent, distant, removed. Nobody knew him here. Hold on. That wasn't quite true. Some remembered his mother. Don't get off on the wrong foot now, he warned himself. The KDA sign was only up a few days. OK, it's down again but you're still in business. You can make a success of this yet, if you wish. If it doesn't work out in the end, so what? Who knows? Give it a chance. It might turn out to be interesting.

But investigating a lost kitten. Would he be the laughing stock of the place? The magpies chatted on.

The good thing about this enterprise is that it doesn't have to succeed. He'd had enough of all that, people climbing all over each other to get to the top. Top of a steaming dung hill. The rat race is over. You're not competing with anybody. It doesn't matter what you solve or don't solve. It's just a hobby. Look on it as nothing more than a spot of gardening. Getting rid of a few weeds. It's all as inconsequential as magpie chatter.

Here in Powl Duv, success or failure mean nothing. In the first place, there aren't going to be too many cases to solve—and did it really matter a damn if he solved them or not? A kitten. Not the best start. He forced himself to give a little smile. A kitten it is then. Better than DNA analysis, better than setting up police protection, better than undercover, better than mounds of paperwork. Handcuffs. He could cuff someone blindfolded, as easily as putting his hands in his pockets. (Not that he ever did. No. But it was part of his training once, before they decided he wasn't destined for the streets, the alleys, the stake outs, the action.) He mightn't have been part of the action but it ended up on his desk nonetheless, second-hand, the blood wiped clean. The fighting subdued. Bullets extracted and sent to the lab. Wasn't it worse than to be in the thick of the action, to read, write, edit, or summarize reports? That's why he had to get out. To escape. Rid himself of a system that had begun to infect him, routines that had dehumanized him. The pain, the sorrow. Not his. No. That of others. You begin to think it's not real. Something happening on a screen. But it seeps through. Gets under your skin and erupts. The trace of sorrow. You can't see it. Others can. Like a boil on the back of your neck.

The reports were nothing but grey seas, oceans of words. Thirty years of slowly growing numb, hour by hour, day by day, week by week, page after page. Once in a while a detail would emerge from the lifeless sea, like a whale or a reef. And he would almost gasp at man's capacity to do evil, man's endless ingenuity. And then nothing but the sea of words again, mouse-grey, unruffled.

He breathed in deeply. The air here would help him think more clearly, see more clearly. Yes, what a tonic it was. Good Atlantic air, sharp and strong, slightly mellowed by autumn decay. This air would add a year or two to his life. Unquestionably. Plus the fact that he had said good-bye to gadgetry and technology. No mobile phones. No computers. No bugs or hidden microphones, not that he had first-hand experience of the latest technology. All he needed now was the bare minimum. One desk phone. A notepad. He would rely on instinct. Instinct and observation. Already he had picked up a hint from May that it would be no harm to learn how to pronounce the names of towns, villages and town lands. He'd go a step further and find out what the names meant. Why not learn the ancestral tongue? No half measures. Go native, my son!

A green van rounded a corner and chugged gingerly along the narrow road. It spluttered once or twice and finally came to a stop. The driver put his greyish head out the window.

"You're the man up above, aren't you?" he asked, looking up at Shane's house.

"I am," said Shane.

The driver pointed his thumb at the sign on the van. POST.

"Michael McCarthy. But everyone calls me Mick the Posht."

"Shane O'Neil."

"Nothin for you today, Mr O'Neil. But 'tis early days yet. We'll give em another few weeks before they start writin to you, will we?"

"Who might they be?" asked Shane, politely.

"Income Tax, who else! Lishten, if there's anythin you want to know about Powl Duv and immediate environs, I'm your man." He looked around, somewhat furtively Shane thought, as though sharing some wild conspiracy.

"I'm what you might call the local historian around here, you see, along with everythin else. That clump of trees over there to your right, about half a mile away?"

"Yes?"

"They call that Dureen so they do. There's a poet buried there. It's all a bit of a mystery really. You might solve it someday if you've nothin better to do."

"Mystery? What kind of mystery?" Shane looked over across the morning fields. A plover cried. Now, how did he know it was a plover? A childhood memory? Was it a plover?

"Was that a plover?" asked Shane?

"It was. The pilibeen they call him here. Now Shane, the mystery of the poet? I'll tell you about it some other time. We'd be all mornin at it if I got started at all. Oh, I don't mean that he was murdered or anythin like that. No, God forbid. You'd never murder a poet if you knew what was good for you. Not around here anyway. God almighty, no! The English hanged a poet once in Killarney, or so I'm told, but your man over in Dureen, no, he wasn't hanged at all. A Gaelic poet he was. The ould folk still have some of his verses. The more south-west you go, the more verses you'll get off them. Drive east from here now and you'll get nothin at all. Not a trace of a whisper. *Faic*, as they say. That means nothin. But you probably know that if you're originally from here. Nothin. Ten miles wesht, on the other hand, and they have some of his love charms." He winked.

Why did you wink?

"Love charms?" Shane was trying to salvage something from this avalanche of words.

"I'll give you one of his charms now and then I'll be gone. I can only give it to you in the English. As you can imagine, there was a lot more power in the Irish because he would have used formulae goin back to the Druids. True as God! I only heard it the once in Irish. From an ould uncle of mine. Put a tingle up my back and down again it did. Holy Mother of God, when I think of it. Here goes anyway: "Mary Mary, put your heart into the buttermilk. Into the buttermilk. Into the buttermilk. Give it a whisk with a hazel twig and drink it all down, drink it all down. A whisssssk—and drink it all down." Whatever it all means. Probably losht a bit in translation. The Irish of it was much longer, of course. And more guttural. *Bláthach*. That's the Irish for buttermilk. You

31

nearly have to churn it around in your mouth all day to say it. I haven't enough teeth left to say it proper. Anyway, the bit I gave you there, that's all they have of it around here. My uncle said it was the Famine that killed off all the love charms. They had more on their minds than love, the poor unfortunates. Your man that's buried beyond, 'twas he came up with the charm I'm after givin you. And he had charms for plenty other things too. Not just love, no siree. He could make himself invisible with them."

Make himself invisible?

"I see. Would you like a mint?"

"A mint? What class of a mint? I'd take a soft one, OK."

Shane pulled out some lint from his trouser pocket.

Damn!

"Sorry. I've run out. You were saying? Oh yes, charms. And people still use these charms, do they?" asked Shane, lightly, as his brain was trying to digest an overload of information and deal with a mint shortage at the same time.

"The invisibility one is gone. Wherever it's gone to. But the love charm? Sure that's the mystery. Is it still around or not? You can't say it out loud, you see. I was just sayin it there to you, you know, so as you'd be able to get a tashte of it. But you wouldn't say it out loud if you were actually usin it to charm someone else. Do you follow me? 'Twouldn't work in yer ordinary voice. Not at all. You'd have to say it maybe an octave higher or even an octave lower, or not with your own voice at all. The way I heard it from my uncle you'd think it wasn't a human sound at all. No, no. Definitely not. A wail from the heart of some kind of animal in the woods. Do you believe in the banshee? We'll talk about her another time. But the love charm, that's part of the whole mystery of the thing, who's sayin it and who's not and them that are sayin it are they sayin it right and all that. Nobody knows for certain if it's being used any more and if you said you heard it people might say you were only hearin things. The wind or somethin comin up from Dureen. I'd say meself the love charm is as strong as ever. And maybe it's used a lot more often than people like to think it is. Even some of the young ones that know nothin do be usin it so they do. And why wouldn't they? OK, I'll be off now."

"Thanks, Mick. Take care. Oh, Mick?"

"Shane?"

"What was I about to say? Oh yes, didn't come across a wee kitten in your travels? White. One black ear?"

Mick's face darkened. He put his hands on the steering wheel.

"One black ear? No," he said and pressed the button to close the window. He started the engine. It spluttered and coughed a bit before coming to life.

Though his head still reeled a bit, Shane was glad that he had now met two of the local characters. May Kelly. Mick the Posht. He waved as Mick went off. The postman didn't return the wave. Preoccupied with something no doubt, thought the detective.

From the PRIVATE DIARY of Shane O'Neill

I'm back again, Miss Diary. Can I call you Miss? I can call you anything I like, I suppose. Of course I can. You are my own private diary. Not some Europol report. You're mine. I own you. I can be nice to you, if I like. Or I can destroy you. Which is it going to be? These words are not answerable to anyone. No Sphinx is going to attack them with her red ink.

What are you, anyway? Just thoughts? My thoughts. And what are they? Are they real? Are they even mine? Do I have any control over them? I sometimes wonder. I'm just recording them here. For myself. I'll destroy them eventually. Oh, yes. Don't get too fond of yourself, Missy. You're just a map to get me wherever it is I'm going and when I get there, that's it. End of story.

Thoughts. I don't know where they come from. Or where they go. How can you know where all your thoughts come from? Can you stop them? Is there a space between two thoughts? Is it the same space for everyone? Or do some people have big gaps between thoughts? What's happening there, in that space, if it is a space? Nothing? Is that what death is like? The space between thoughts, except that instead of lasting a second or a minute it lasts for an eternity... or until the next thought begins to think it's time to emerge. To stir itself. Into existence. For a minute. From where? A void? And when a thought has come and gone, where does it go? Into a thought bank? What is a thought anyway? Some kind of electric activity inside the brain? Can you have a thought without a brain?

❖

OK. This is good, Shane. Go on. Write it all down. Have a conversation with yourself. There wasn't anybody in The Hague to talk to about such things. Forget The Hague, will you? I have. It's forgotten.

OK, it will come up now and again—maybe when you least expect it—but it's all over and done with now. No need to revisit.

Just checking that things are OK. The transition. The change in my life. The return to my roots. So far so good, I suppose. The usual gaffes. The mints are a help. I must say. I'd be lost without them. It all came to me one morning. A whole system. By sucking or chewing a mint, you get time to collect your thoughts. You don't have to blurt out something stupid or explode or look dumb and regret it afterwards. The sucking or gentle chewing has a calming effect, on yourself and on others, and the all-important factor is that you have a few seconds before answering a question. It's a matter of timing. Making it look natural. Not a quick grab for a mint if asked something that might be a bit tricky. A natural movement. Also, offering someone a mint is a way of breaking the ice, showing you are a thoughtful, considerate person. Watch how a cow chews the cud. It's very unthreatening.

You offered a mint to the Sphinx one morning. And she accepted. That was a good start. On the second morning she refused. But maybe she wasn't a minty person and had only accepted the first time out of politeness. Or was it that the second time was going too far in the relationship between minion and master? People pretended to be equals. Democracy and all that. We are feudal.

There's a book in this mint business. I could make a mint! If I could get a ghost writer to write it for me. The Minty Way. Great title. The cover has smiling, attractive persons on it. A section on how a minty breath, a fresh breath, is an important social asset. Building up slowly to the way you can use the mint for relaxing effects. A section on dividing society up into those who are pro-mint and anti-mint. Make the anti-mint crowd a bit sinister or inferior in some way. It might work. People who write such books are considered authorities on their subjects. We could have seminars and workshops and all sorts of things. Maybe here, in Kerry. In a hotel in Tralee, or Killarney. Or Dingle. Suck Your Way to Confidence. That would supplement your pension nicely, wouldn't it? Mints! Stop it. As they say here in Kerry, "You're a bit of a mintal case!" Focus! Focus! Focus! Forget the mints. Money corrupts.

35

It's the KDA, right? Don't get distracted. KDA all the way. Say it. KDA all the way. Chant it. Start the day with the KDA. Wake up every morning to that mantra. Go to sleep with it. Write it in big letters. Fine. Now write it on the top of every page in this diary. KDA all the way? I'm sounding like a US marine. What time is it? I must go to bed. The night air is poisoning my brain, the air from Dureen.

No. Keep at it. Keep on writing. Get it all down. For Your Eyes Only, so write anything you like. OK then, so, how are things? Not bad. Sleeping better than ever, most nights. Must be the air. Day-air. Night-air tricky.

Eyes still adjusting, though. Sometimes I think I see a rabbit or a hare in the distant fields. Can't be sure. And ears? Ears can't get used to the silence. It's like an ocean. You want to dive into it. Make a splash. An ocean of silence.

Things loom out of the silence. Awful things. Things studied in myriad reports, reappearing now out of context. Imagining I was there, in the thick of things. Photographs. From every angle. I can see it all now, again, as I did then.

Of course it would slow you down, what did they expect, that I swallow all these horrendous details? I couldn't help imagining the incident, piecing it together in my mind. Jigsaw of evil. And if the report somehow came together with no large gaps or inconsistencies, it would pass out of my hands and disappear. I'd never see it again. It was looking for gaps that slowed me down. As well as gremlins in the computer.

Farewell forever to Raamweg 47! Only four people turned up on the day. I'd say they were roped in. A lot of shuffling of feet. I shuffled too. (I'm still shuffling.)

I was going to retire anyway, even before the psychologist's report. What a nonsense, what did that prove? Nothing. It just said I needed a change. Bloody sure I did. Since there wasn't anything suitable they could offer, would I consider early retirement. Of course I would. Jumped at it. Who wouldn't? And then—you clear your desk and leave it clean and tidy for the next person and you walk out the door. Without looking back. And you've taken nothing with you. No favourite mug. No photo of a dear one. You've left the desk more or less as you found it.

What could you have possibly left behind that might be of any value? A paper clip? A stapler?

Whither?

Couldn't stay in The Hague. Nothing for me there, or anywhere else in Europe for that matter. Then things began to fall into place. Who knows, had I left it any longer this house might not be standing. I'd have come back to rubble.

❖

May Kelly. Is she sound in the head? I suppose she is. Harmless old thing. Mick the Posht? Never came across anyone like him before. He wouldn't last a week in The Hague. They'd lock him up. Was he acting? Must observe more. Do people here behave the same way among their own as they behave with me? I sometimes think they're putting on some kind of an act for me. Don't know exactly why. To amuse me? Impress me? I'll say, "I'm not amused," next time. No, better not. No smart stuff.

I suppose I'm acting as well. Taking myself a bit too seriously. What was that fella called, Walter Mitty? Living in an imaginary world he was. But who can draw the line between real and imaginary? A lot of stuff that happens it's so strange you couldn't make it up, you couldn't imagine it. So, the divide can't be all that clear, can it? Nothing is black and white. Look at science. First you see these devices in a James Bond film. Next thing you know, they're real. In the real world. The world is imitating Hollywood. What was imagined is becoming real, concrete. Didn't it say so in the paper the other day. Scientists now able to create an Invisible Man. An Invisible Man. What a detective he'd make! There is no distinction between real and imaginary any more.

Stop! Stop this line of questioning for good. Create your own past. Believe in it. I am Shane O'Neil. I am not a fake. I am not a liar. I am not an impostor. If I'm an impostor, everyone's an impostor. How about

37

that? The Pope is an impostor. I'm Shane O'Neil. KDA. Kerry Detective Agency. It's as simple as that. Like it or lump it. That's what they say around here. Like it or lump it. I like it. OK? Is that OK with everyone? Everyone happy? Good. KDA, all the way!

❖

Love charms! Did you ever hear the like! They'd look at you in a funny way if you brought up love charms in Raamweg 47. They'd send for the men in white coats.

❖

Strangest bloody dream ever. If you could call it a dream. I woke up and closed my eyes again or half closed them and saw myself as a female. Lying down in bed.

My legs apart. Giving birth. And a figure standing by the bed—the poet, was it, the poet that's buried in Dureen Wood? He was in the middle of an incantation. I'm giving birth—to myself! And the poet, I don't understand what he's saying, but it appears he's welcoming me into the world. This can't be. And I hear a cry. It's me, my first cry.

My mother was the sun, my father the moon.

—Dutch Diaries (destroyed) of Shane O'Neil

Chapter 3

The Cat's Pyjamas

"**M**r O'Neil?"

"Speaking."

"The Cat's Pyjamas."

"Sorry?"

"The Cat's Pyjamas. We're a small publisher here in Tralee. With the emphasis on *small*."

"Yes?"

"Well, we were thinking—my name is Brian Smith by the way."

"Hello." Has this Smith fellow been reading my Diary? Is he interested in The Minty Way? Shane needed a mint.

"Hello? Are you there?"

"Yes. Sorry. Just... chewing something. You might... you might have an idea what I'm chewing, perhaps?"

"An apple? No? Well, I'm not the detective. You are, Shane. Can I call you Shane? Listen, we've heard you've moved into Powl Duv and all that and we're always looking out for—you know, someone said you were with Interpol. Is that right?"

"Correct. And Europol."

"Amazing. Look, I'll get to the point. Would you be interested in writing your memoirs for The Cat's Pyjamas? I mean, like, sorry, I nearly choked on a pretzel there. Excuse me. Sorry about that. Pretzels! Far from pretzels we were reared! Hah? Where was I? Like, we're not huge or anything and there wouldn't be much money in it, I'm afraid but...

MY HEAD IS MISSING

we're really anxious to diversify, you know, and well, next time you're in Tralee, would you give us a shout and we could, like, sit down and maybe talk about it? Or go out and have a couple of pints. Or skinny lattes? Hello? Mr O'Neil? Like, you wouldn't have to write it yourself, like, if you didn't want to. We've one or two ghost writers lined up in Listowel like, you know. Just, like, to get your story down, you know? I do a bit of ghostin myself as well. Kerry themes. You might have seen our book about how to win prizes at Writers' Week Listowel? Sold very well that one. Another one about mushroom picking in North Kerry. That didn't sell brilliant, between yourself and myself, but we've one or two hot ones in the pipeline. I'll say no more about those for the moment. Sure, all books don't have to come from Dublin or Cork now, do they? I'm telling you, we're as good as them fellas any day. We get a few grants too you know, to encourage regionalization, which isn't a bad thing is it? Anyways, I've said enough. I'll say no more. I'm really looking forward to meeting you. What do you say? Will we talk about it?"

Shane sighed and put down the phone. He didn't want to talk about it.

From the PRIVATE DIARY of Shane O'Neil

What did Brian Smith want? What was he expecting? Car chases in Amsterdam, Hamburg, Milan? Please! More bullet points than bullets, I'm afraid. Imagine if I had agreed to meet with this Smith fella and was lured into telling him some cock and bull story. How long before they'd find out? Of course, if I used a pseudonym? I should have thought of that. No, that wouldn't work. They'll only publish the book if they can link it with a real detective, living here in Powl Duv. Local interest. That's what sells. A photo of a man walking the quiet leafy little roads around Powl Duv, a man that was involved in life-threatening car chases through the streets of Berlin, Bucharest, Bilbao. Sure. It would be a hell of a good feature in the *Kerryman* to promote the book but, no, they're not going to publish a pack of lies. You can't be involved in car chases if you don't even drive a car. Maybe that's why I never got promoted. Leave him tied to the desk. Poor man, never even learned to drive.

❖

Car chases! There wasn't much excitement around my desk in Raamweg 47 if the truth be told. Spilling a cup of coffee. Would you like to read about that, Mr Brian Smith, whoever you are? In the course of a long career with Interpol and later with Europol, Shane O'Neil shares his secrets with us and reckons he must have spilled ten or even twelve cups of coffee a year. Is that exciting enough for you? Man used four thousand paper clips in course of uneventful career. Try to sell that story, Mr Smith.

❖

Finally picked up enough courage to look through an old dictionary. I'm underlining some Irish words that are stranger to me than fiction. I wonder if they are still in use? Probably not. If I write out the words

43

and the definition in my diary, I might remember them better. Getting a chance to use them is another question.

> "*Gabhairín*: pronounced GOWER-EEN: potatoes sold secretly for pocket-money."

Secretly? It's all so strange. But this must be well over a hundred years ago. What if some of these words are still in use? Not around Powl Duv, that's for sure.

> "*Seicimín*: pronounced SHEK-IMEEN: the belly-skin that falls down, in well-fed geese, between the legs."
> "*Iomas gréine*: pronounced UM-ASS GRAY-NE: sun-inspiration, a sun-bubble caused on herbs which if eaten gives the gift of poetry."

What herbs exactly? Looks like the dictionary is deliberately tantalizing.

> "*Seala:* pronounced SHALL-AH: a ration of four eggfulls of honey."

Unbelievable!

❖

I wonder why they called this place Powl Duv? Maybe "powl" or "poll" means more than just a hole?

> "Poll... pronounced POWL to rhyme with Fowl: a hole, a pit, a hollow, an orifice, puncture, a bog-hole, a deep part of a river, a breach, a rent in a garment, the connecting link of a rosary beads..."

Strange words, strange meanings. A word should mean one thing, not another. Maybe that's it, a war of words is a war of worlds. Someone believes something to mean a certain thing and someone else says it means something else. These words and definitions do not reflect what it is to be a human being in today's society, do they? Should they be allowed to die a natural death? Or can we breathe life into them again? *Iomas gréine*. A sun bubble that turns you into a poet if you eat it? Sounds like a Druidic ritual. What exactly is a sun bubble? A sun-bubble caused on herbs. What herbs? It doesn't say. It's just a dictionary. It's not a book of spells. Anyway, better look out for those sun-bubbles whatever they are. Don't want to turn into a poet. We've problems enough as it is.

The Cat's Pyjamas. Looking for writers, are they? Why don't they just give out herbs with sun-bubbles on them?

There is a rose without a thorn.

—Dutch Diaries (destroyed) of Shane O'Neil

Chapter 4

The Country's Gone to the Dogs

Fifty years ago, when he was a young lad, you'd be lucky if you got a ham sandwich in a rural pub. Ireland has changed, mused Shane, as he raised another spoonful of thick chowder to his lips. Clams. People shunned them in days gone by, he was told. A sign of poverty, a throwback to the Famine when hungry hordes headed for the shores. And food being exported from the country at gunpoint. But not for their mouths. One evening, as the sun went down over Dureen he thought he saw them—waifs, wandering ghosts on the road. Starvelings. Hoping to reach the shore and find a clam.

Only the other day he had read in a newspaper that a clam was taken from the sea a hundred miles from the Kerry coast. It was four hundred years old—and still alive. Could that be true?

He had only patchy memories of Ireland from his boyhood days. Before his mother's early death. Before he was taken away. Memories wiped out, or buried deeper than where that old clam was found. He remembered, vaguely, that a pub was always a very smoky, noisy place. Games of cards or darts. Or rings. The sound of the rubber ring as it landed on the hook. What else? A roaring fire. Ballads galore. "There was a wild colonial boy, Jack Duggan was his name..."

Changed utterly. And what a colourful jigsaw it had now become! Places like Powl Duv would rarely if ever be darkened by a stranger. Now he was being served by an East European. Could be Latvian. Or Polish.

"Anything else, Sir?"

"Coffee, please. By the way, didn't see a stray kitten by any chance?"

"Kitten? What is kitten?"

"I'm looking for a kitten. Pussy?"

"Ah, sex-kitten? Here no. You must go to Tralee for that. You want number? I give you number."

Shane got up.

"Forget the coffee," he said. Leaving a tenner on the table, he walked out of the pub.

The air had changed. Was it going to rain? He passed May's B & B. A sign saying VACANCIES in one of the windows. There was something very old-fashioned about the font and he remembered posters from his youth, one of them advertising a circus. By all appearances May had no guests at all.

"It will!" She was standing in the doorway, smoking.

What? "It will what?"

"Rain!"

Could she read his thoughts? He came nearer.

"Or then again it mightn't. It might pass over. But it rarely does. And Bella out there somewhere in this weather. If she's alive at all. What are we supposed to do? I hear Satanism has come to Ireland now. That's what they're sayin. A man from Moyvane said it on the radio. He's usually fairly reliable."

Ever since he arrived back in Ireland—or, more specifically, Kerry— Shane had been half-enjoying such non sequiturs: things didn't follow the usual logical pattern; people launched into tirades, or musings, or fantasies, reams of speech without any warning; many of these monologues were disjointed, at least to his ears, leaping from one thing to another. Quite a number of mints needed to be sucked or chewed or played with under the tongue to get through it all. Language was a frantic deer, pursued by fairy hounds.

"Satanism?"

"Animal sacrifices. Cats burned to death. Dunkeys. The country's gone to the dogs. I'll tell you, if one of them Satanists lays a finger on my Bella, I'll send him straight back to hell with smoke comin out of his rear end, so I will." She crunched the cigarette under her heel.

"You'll keep a look out for them, Mr O'—Shane, won't you?"

"I will, May."

She smiled broadly. Her teeth weren't great. Uneven. Yellowish. But at least she smiled. His former colleagues in Interpol, why did they fork out so much money on their teeth? They never smiled.

"I will to be sure."

Whether consciously or not, he was beginning to remember how his mother spoke—her rhythms, phrases or snatches of sentences, the gentle melody of her voice. I'll be speaking like the good denizens of Powl Duv before long—or close enough to it. But will I ever be able to speak with all of my mother's inflections? His syllables, when he paused to listen to them, internally, or spoken, were not naturally soothing. His voice could never become an affectionate voice, a healing voice. If the truth be told, after her death he spoke very little for a long, long time and when he did begin to speak again his own voice sounded distant, the voice of another.

The sky spat a few drops. He looked up. That was about it, a drop or two: it didn't look like a shower. He strolled at an even pace and allowed the greenness of fields and trees to colour his thoughts. What would the world be without green? A nightmarish, alien world, surely, a dog-eat-dog world.

Nettles. A few blackberries. Some lonesome-looking ragworts in a field. Colours, shapes, textures. He was taking them all in. There was something comforting even in the stinging nettle. Seeing it again. Recognizing it. The shape. The colour. Remembering the sting. He could remember the sting of a nettle. But it must be nearly half a century ago!

The light from the sky, silvery and liquid through golden leaves, sometimes shimmering, darting or flickering on and off, or obeying the whims of the wind. An advance army of clouds slowly coming in from the Atlantic, soon to take over the whole of Ireland. The world was alive and he was entering that life, blinking, emerging after a long hibernation.

When he got back he poured himself a drop of buttermilk. He didn't much like the look of it. As soon as he put it to his lips he knew it had soured. Suddenly there was a ring. Somebody had pressed the door bell and was letting it ring like a fire alarm. Shane went to the door, annoyed at the prolonged ringing. He was surprised to see a policeman and a bright, young, attractive bangharda by his side.

"You'd be O'Neil, then?"

"Come in," said Shane.

"We're not here to socialize, Mr O'Neil. Could I see your licence please?"

"What licence would that be, Sergeant?"

"WHAT? It's not a TV licence we're after."

"Good. I don't have a TV."

The young bangharda looked at the sergeant, a little nervously.

"Snooper's licence!" he thundered, the unexpected explosion ending in a sneer that he had difficulty maintaining.

"One moment, Sergeant," said Shane, feigning politeness, and went to fetch his documents. The bangharda was about to take them from Shane when the sergeant snapped them.

"Hmmm," he muttered after a while. "Seems to be in order. Get your certificate framed and shtick it on the wall, will you?"

Then he stared at Shane. Steely blue eyes. The eyes of an interrogator. Shane stared back at him. Was this going to be a staring match? He had trained people in this game, staring until the eyes burned in your head. Well, not really. But he had fantasized about it, for hours on end. The bangharda looked shyly at her feet.

"You didn't introduce yourself, Sergeant..." said Shane eventually.

"Listen, O'Neil, and listen very carefully to me now, me boyo." His face was becoming redder and a protruding vein in his forehead throbbed angrily. The redness contrasting with the whites of his eyes. "We don't like snoopers or soupers or poopers in Kerry. Do you have me now? We had one of your fellas in Tralee a while back. The man was a liability, if you follow me. Do you know what I'm sayin? A bit of a pest. Stickin his nose where it didn't belong. Do you hear what I'm tellin you? That's not our way around here in the Kingdom. Do you get my drift?" The sergeant shifted from one leg to another, as if both legs were paining him, or as if he needed to urinate.

Should I ask him does he need to use the toilet?

"*Mi casa tu casa*, Sergeant," blurted Shane. It was a phrase he had picked up a few years ago from watching a favourite film at least a dozen times.

"WHAT?" The sergeant came closer to Shane and peered into his eyes as though the translation was there staring him right in the face, in subtitles.

The bangharda coughed. Without looking at her, the sergeant registered his annoyance that she had broken some evil spell he was trying to work on Shane.

"Nothing. No. Yes. I mean, I get your drift, Sergeant."

"You do, do you? Well, we're the law around here, O'Neil. An Garda Síochána. That's us." He pointed to the bangharda and to himself, as if there might be some doubt about the matter.

"You? You're nothin. Do you understand? Nothin at all."

"Right, Sergeant, I'll remember that."

"You're just a blow-in from foreign parts, so be careful."

Blow-in? I'm not going to let you get away with that.

"Actually, Sergeant, my people came down from the North the time of the Battle of Kinsale. They got frozen in on their way back and for some reason or other they settled down here in Powl Duv. Must be well over four hundred years ago."

The sergeant pursed his lips, as though intent on exploding, or breaking wind. Shane reached into his pocket.

"Would either of you care for a mint?"

The sergeant gave him a withering look and turned on his heels.

"*Zoon van een hoerige kameel*," muttered Shane.

The sergeant turned round.

"WHAT?"

"Nothing. Talking to myself, Sergeant."

The bangharda looked at him. Did Shane imagine that she quickly mimed the word "Sorr-y" to excuse the boorishness of her boss?

She and the sergeant took off.

What was all that about? He shuddered. Not that he felt bullied by the sergeant. He was almost impervious to crude behaviour. Had seen too much of it. It was just that it wasn't what he expected to happen in Powl Duv. Then again, what had he expected? What had he dreamed? What had he hoped for? Nothing. A rest. A long rest. Oblivion. Why had he called the sergeant the son of a hairy camel? He had never used that phrase before. And I don't mind if I never use it again, he thought.

The police car roared off. A flock of some thirty or so crows blackened the sky. Sucking a mint, he watched the world. He would never let the world sour his life again, he would never allow himself to go stale or feel useless or inferior. Never again. His tongue played with the mint until there was nothing left of it.

It began to rain. He had also promised himself to listen to music every day. All sorts of music. Opera. Jazz. Traditional Irish music. Sacred music. Choirs. He put on the radio, moved the dial until he found LYRIC FM, sat down and listened to some Gilbert and Sullivan. It was slightly inane but it lightened his mood. One of his techniques for what he called mental hygiene was to imagine someone hateful or repugnant as something else entirely, a slight figure wandering all alone in a Chinese landscape—a wallpaper image from a Chinese restaurant that had stayed with him—or a clown in a circus. And now he imagined the sergeant not as one of those figures, less potent now due to overuse, but as a whole chorus of skittish girls from the Gilbert and Sullivan operetta he was listening to:

> Twenty love-sick maidens we,
> Love-sick all against our will.
> Twenty years hence, we shall be
> Twenty love sick maidens still...

There! Gone! Completely transmogrified. What a technique. He had first used it on his superior, his adversary, the Sphinx. She had become various things, a cat, a parrot, a shrimp. For one whole month she was a chimpanzee. Things were fine until he tossed her a peanut. That needed some explanation.

Turning off the radio, he took down a book about the Skelligs. Was this what retirement was all about, listening to the radio, reading books? Well, why not? He corrected himself: semi-retirement.

Leafing through the book his eye fell on a quote from George Bernard Shaw:

> Yesterday I left the Kerry coast in an open boat, 33 feet long, propelled by ten men on five oars. These men started on 49 strokes a minute, a rate which I did not believe they could keep up for five minutes. They kept it without slackening half a second for two hours, at the end of which they landed me on the most fantastic and impossible rock in the world: Skellig Michael, or the Great Skellig, where in south west gales the spray knocks stones out of the lighthouse keeper's house, 160 feet above calm sea level...

He had nodded off and dreamed of gannets. Thousands of them nesting where the monks of old had their bee-hive huts on the Great Skellig. No radio or trashy novels for them. The crash of waves below, the cry of birds above and all around, incessant cries to God their maker.

He got up slowly, stretched himself, walked over to the window and looked out. An army of stars stretching away into infinity. Awaiting orders. He stood there. He had often watched the stars as a child and wondered were they friendly. Or indifferent? Did they watch over us? Now he merely marvelled at their brightness. He had lived in cities for so long that he had almost forgotten what darkness was like. Silky darkness. The studded heavens.

Well, said Shane to himself, nothing in the house but sour buttermilk. I'll pop down to the pub for a stew or something. I'll leave the radio on. It will be a welcoming sound when I return.

The air was keen. A star had lodged neatly in a wet pothole and winked up at Shane as he strolled by. He began to whistle Gilbert and Sullivan. That always happens. Whenever he listens to a familiar tune he finds himself whistling or humming it at some later stage, when the music has stopped.

Outside O'Dea's stood a little wizened man, a remnant from half-forgotten days with his frayed tweed waistcoat and peak cap, both of which had seen better times, a man with little of the world to claim his own and even less still to desire.

"Evenin to you!" said he, taking his pipe out of his mouth and looking at it as though he had never seen it before.

"Shane O'Neil."

"I know well who you are. Cherokee Jim. From Skrahancockgower. That's what they call me anyway."

"Why is that?" asked Shane.

"The time of the smokin ban. I told them I'd smoke wherever, whatever and whenever I liked. Wasn't I a Cherokee? Part of my religion it was. To smoke the ould peace pipe."

"Good one that. What happened?"

"They just laughed. At first. Then I got on page three of the *Kerryman*. The headline said 'Put That in Your Pipe says Cherokee Jim from Skrahan'. A lot of people thought I was makin a fool out of Kerry. I wasn't. What eejit would try make a fool out of the Kingdom? If you ask me it was the *Kerryman* what was makin a fool out of itself. I don't buy it anymore. Sure if there's anythin in it someone will tell me all about it. What would I want to be buyin it for? I buy real toilet paper now with aloe vera in it. Very kind to the ould posterior it is too. Anyways, the law said, prove it, me bucko. Prove you're a Cherokee. That was the hard part. I rattled off a few phrases to Sergeant O'Brien—some ould things I heard me grandfather sayin once: *kneel ane law day naw fine lauma nogger*—stuff like that and sure he said that could be Irish or Latin. So I was shtuck. Prove it's not Cherokee says I. No, no, the onus is on you, is what they said. Didn't have Cherokee papers.

Had to pay the fine. And a hefty fine it was too. Nearly wiped me out so it did."

"Well, at least you tried..."

"Where did it get me? It put O'Dea's pub here on the map for a wee while, so it did, and I got the odd *taoscán* of whiskey on the house. But I had to sell a small field to pay the fine. The field next to the field where the Heapies were last summer."

"Heapies?"

"Fellas with long hair and golden girls that are laughin all the time and takin their clothes off whenever it's hot. Heapies. They found a circle in me other wee field in Skrahancockgower and they all came and danced around it. Faith, I danced around it meself. They said they'll be back next summer and that they'd bring me a piece of paper makin me an honorary Cherokee. The only piece of paper I have is my birth certificate. It would be nice to add to the collection..." He coughed and spat like a man who'd rather spit into a spittoon than into the empty night.

"The smoke'll be the death of me. I mightn't be here at all when the Heapies come back. Best crowd of people that ever came to the Kingdom of Kerry. Though not everyone would agree with me on that score. The *Kerryman* ran a campaign agin them. But don't let me delay you. I'll be talkin to you agin!"

"You will. By the way, what's the meaning of Skrahancockgower?" He mentally clapped himself on the back for pronouncing it successfully.

"Somethin to do with goats' shit. Cock gower. No goats there now. A Belgian shot them all. Every single one of them. Made bodhráns out of their shkins, or so I'm told, and sold the mate to the Moroccans. Belgian fella. I'll tell you his name in a minute."

Cherokee looked up and his mouth opened as though he had seen an angel in the sky. Shane had no interest whatsoever in the Belgian's name but waited politely.

"Gezelle was his name. I knew I'd think of it because it's like the animal."

"Oh yes, gazelle."

"Except he was Gezelle with an 'e' in it. When he ran out of goats he started shootin horses so he did. That's when they caught up with him."

"Horses?"

"Maybe he was doin em a favour. People were lettin horses go. Hundreds of em. The upkeep was too much."

Did this fellow—who must be well into his seventies—did he actually walk here?

"And do you walk it here from Skrahancockgower?"

"I do. And back."

"Must be over two miles."

"It's the best part of three Irish miles, so it is. I stopped on the way for to water the weeds—well, you'll never believe it!"

"What?"

He took his pipe out of his mouth and looked at it, tenderly.

"Didn't the sergeant see me. Stopped his car and got out. He was eatin a cheeseburger. I was about to tell him not to be drivin and eatin at the same time but he got in before me. Cherokee, says he, there are designated areas for smokin your pipe and there are designated areas for relievin yerself and this is not a designated area, says he. And is it a designated area for cheeseburgers, says I. I'll take none of your ould lip, says he. Ever since the sergeant was the target of a flyin horseshoe during the Rose of Tralee week, three years ago this comin August, he's been a bit soft in the head. Designated area, is it? Do you know what, I'll tell you somethin for nothin': the whole of Ireland will be designated before long. You won't be able to blow your nose or wink at a girl except in designated areas. If I live to see 2016 and the anniversary of the Risin, I'm goin to go straight up to the post office in Dublin and have meself a bit of an uprisin so I am. The way I see it, we'll have to start all over agin."

"And I'll be with you!"

"Please God and you might!"

Shane looked at him and said to himself he wouldn't be surprised if Cherokee lived to see the hundredth anniversary of the Rising.

"Do you walk here every day? That's a terrible long walk."

"Couldn't afford to come here every day. No, Sir. Whenever the Spirit moves me."

"You're sounding like a proper Cherokee now."

"Tell that to the paleface sergeant in Tralee!"

The barman-cum-pimp was still on duty in O'Dea"s.

"I have long Polish name. No one here pronounce. They call me Thady. You call me Thady too."

"OK Thady Too, that's what I'll call you," chuckled Shane. "And I'm Shane."

"What am I getting you? O'Dea's Famous Stew comes highly recommended." He said it like a formula, or a line of verse learned by rote.

"That's what I'll have then," said Shane without further ado. He was famished and didn't feel like wasting too much time bantering with O'Dea's famous Thady Too.

"You will not regret it," says Thady. "It also have parsnips in it."

He collected a few empty glasses and kicked the kitchen door open. Shane guessed that Thady was cook, kitchen porter, plumber, electrician and devil-knows-what-else all rolled into one. This was confirmed on his return ten minutes later.

"O'Deas they are in Turkey. Only me here. They have house in Turkey. Near Virgin Mary House. They out there praying in hail, rain and sunshine. Mostly sunshine. I here in Powl Duv, cooking, waiting, washing, everything. Not bad life. But if I get sick. Who does work? Virgin Mary? Enjoy O'Dea's Famous Stew."

"Thank you, Thady. I'm sure I will."

Yes, indeed, it had parsnips in it. Why he bothered to mention them was a mystery to Shane. Were they a rarity in Poland?

He had finished his last morsel when Thady appeared to collect the plate.

"Is there much to do around here, Thady?"

"In Powl Duv? You joking. Nothing. Nothing here. This is time-warp country. Hasn't moved on. All of Ireland move on. Powl Duv not move. No school. No church. You must go to Tralee if you want Mass. Also Mass available in Polish. You need fun? You go to Tralee for fun.

Greyhound racing? Good fun. Discos? Fun. Rose of Tralee, ah! Some day I marry a Rose. If not, go back to Poland. Open up burger joint. Recession, you know. Lots of Poles going home now. Thady's Famous Burger Bistro. Might work, no?"

"Might," said Shane.

"Drink on house?"

"No thanks."

He left a large tip as a contribution to Thady's dream.

"Looks like you last customer," he said. It was only ten o'clock.

"I put up CLOSED sign now and go to bed. Mr and Mrs O'Dea will not know. You tell them nothing, Shane?"

"I'll say nothing, Thady Too!"

From the **PRIVATE DIARY** of Shane O'Neill

It's official now. Kerry Detective Agency. Recognized as such by the long arm of the law. What was it about the sergeant that was so disconcerting? His eyes! Sanpaku eyes! That's it!

Cherokee Jim, I took to him a lot. I'd have liked to have had a father in that mould. Easy going but sharp behind it all. Wry wit. And knowledge. I bet he's a storehouse of arcane knowledge. I'd like to get more out of him. More local lore. History. You need history here. Plenty of it. You can't live without it, without referencing to it.

❖

"*Gealach*: light, moonlight, the moon, frenzy, madness. The white circle in a slice of half-boiled potato."

Very odd. Very, very, very odd.

"*Bearadóir*: a prober; one who probes for bog-wood by means of an iron bar or spike with a wooden handle, the prober having stuck the bar into the bog applies his teeth to the timber handle to detect the bog-wood."

What's going on here?

"*Conach*: the elephant moth, found in dark places and regarded with aversion; on being discovered it is instantly killed as it is believed to sting cattle severely in the muzzle; the ass is supposed to kill it."

But what does it look like? Would Cherokee know?
What is all this stuff? It's not another language, it's another universe.
Reminder: go to Tralee for more mints.

❖

How did it get into the house? Where was it before now? A spider has crept into a crevice in the fireplace with an air of "I've been doing this for a thousand years."

A little black wiggly thing from nowhere, as if it had spun itself out of the night. If there were no fireplace, if this house had crumbled, where would that spider be tonight? In another house? In May Kelly's? Does May keep spiders or, for the sake of her occasional guests, must she squash or swat anything that moves or buzzes or wriggles?

When did you arrive, spider? How long will you stay? Are you setting up a family here? Are we alone? Are we alone together, you and me, spider? How can you be alone? You don't live on air, do you? Soon you'll spin a web to catch something. Right? Good luck! I hope you find something. A wife, maybe?

What have I found? The great detective of Powl Duv. Nothing. Then again, I've found you, spider. (Or you've found me.) I'll be keeping an eye on you.

Listening to a corncrake on the computer, it's not the same thing.

—Dutch Diaries (destroyed) of Shane O'Neil

Chapter 5

Death in Dureen

Shane dreamed the sound of shrill sirens. They wouldn't stop. Half sitting up in bed, reaching for a gun that wasn't there, he soon realized that what had torn him from sleep was not a siren but a crowing cock. *Well, now that I'm awake I might as well get up. The cock was crowing deliberately, with some evil intent. How long has it been? How long since I've heard a cock crowing? Why did I reach for a gun, by the way? I've never had a gun. A pen, Shane, that's all you've ever wielded. A lousy pen.*

Lathering himself with shaving foam, he then took the blade to his neck, paused and began to shave to the exact rhythm of the cock—cock-a-doodle-doo! He reflected on other sounds he had not heard in many a long year. Ducks. Geese. The corncrake. Braying of an ass. To those that hear them every day they are just sounds, background noise, scarcely heard at all. But to Shane—who hadn't heard them for many a long year—for most of his lifetime—something stirred in him when he pondered the loss of such sounds. Sounds that once defined him and his world. Losing them was to lose definition, the contours and acoustics of reality, of an unbroken universe. So deeply had he missed these rustles, squawks, bleatings, buzzes, yelps, neighings, cries that it was only on hearing the cock crow now that its savage beauty was revealed to him in all its perfection. The distant lowing of a cow. And then the cock again. *Let him crow—go on, crow your head off!*

He looked at himself while shaving. Was he more relaxed? Perhaps. Who knows? Happier? Too soon to say. His thoughts were still preoccupied with sounds from his early years. There were more sounds. More sounds, waiting. Not until he heard them would he know what effect they might have on him. And there are buried sounds too, he said, sounds I'll hear no more. If men were to occupy other planets, he mused, would they bring a vast range of natural sounds with them? Goats and geese. Dogs and horses on Mars? But what good is the sound of a goat without a goat?

He fantasized on these matters for a while and then he put the kettle on. A nippy morning. He peered into the grate. What was he supposed to do with the cold ashes? There were lots of details to his new life that had to be filled in. He stared once more at the grate. "*Aingeal*," he said out loud. What was that? He said it again. Was it an Irish word? A word from the past?

With a steaming cup of coffee in his hand, he looked out to see what kind of a day it was. Autumnal mist. No horizon. Had the sky overheard the charm for invisibility and uttered it innocently? A figure with a greyhound was walking briskly towards the little wood known as Dureen. Mick the Posht? He had not seen the full length of him—only his head and shoulders that time in the van—but something told him it had to be Mick. It was Saturday, wasn't it? Yes. He wouldn't be on his postal rounds. Shane felt he had to talk to him. About what, he couldn't rightly say. Suss him out. If he's the local historian, as he claims to be, then Shane needed to know everything there was to know about this village he now called home. Who's who. And who better than the postman to initiate him into the mystery of topography: for a start, he had to be able to pronounce place-names correctly and gather something of their history.

He walked towards Dureen. The figure ahead of him looked left and right and then, patting the dog on the head before rubbing its left ear vigorously, he turned right, into the wood. Shane followed, some distance behind. When he came to the edge of the wood, something inside him told him to be cautious, to avoid being seen. He could see the figure clearly now. Mick the Posht. Another man was standing about twenty yards from him holding a wicker cage. Mick's black greyhound was straining at the leash. The other man opened the cage and a kitten jumped out. On seeing the greyhound it scampered off in a panic. Mick released the hound. Within seconds it was all over.

Shane closed his eyes. Screams he had heard before. Hours of screaming. Squeals. Growls. Shrieks. Sobs. Well, they were in the reports if you knew how to read between the lines. Did he not see everything, hear everything, just as if he'd been there? Blood he had seen before. Rivers of it. Human blood. His own. As a child, his buttocks beaten so hard he had bled. Bled so much that he was sent to the infirmary for nine days.

He knew well what was going on. There was a letter in the paper about it not so long ago. This was a practice among unscrupulous dog-owners, whether theirs were fighting dogs or racing dogs. The theory was that a greyhound would never be truly hungry for victory if it didn't taste the blood of a live victim once in a while.

It was dark in the little wood. He could hear the men laughing. The other man was now standing beside Mick. Could it—? Could it be the sergeant from Tralee? Impossible to tell. Same height. Same build. If he spied on them any longer he might be spotted. What then? Shane slunk out onto the road and back towards home. His head buzzing. Did he regret not having a camera? No, photos can be tampered with and are no longer reliable evidence.

He had to talk to May. But not face to face. Not yet. He would phone her. Later. First he needed a shower. A hot shower. As hot as bearable.

❖

"Hello? It's me, May. Shane."

"You've found her!"

"What? No, May—" He paused. Was he getting soft? Wasn't he once given the bizarre duty of informing a widow that her husband had been decapitated, and it hadn't been in an accident. A samurai sword. No you didn't inform the widow! Not exactly. He had read a report about it, or edited it. He couldn't remember. Anyway, why can't he break the news about a kitten? Damn it, what was her name again?

"May, do you by any chance know what the word *aingeal* means?"

"*Aingeal*? I do. It's Irish for an angel. Why?"

"An angel?"

"An angel. Yes. Where did you hear it?"

"I just—I thought, maybe, I remembered it. Could it be a word my mother had? "

"I don't know. That's not why you rang is it?"

"No." He paused.

"Shane?"

What was the name of her kitten? He racked his brains.

"Shane?"

"I'm here."

"You've found her? You've found Bella?"

Bella, of course!

"Bella's dead, May. Sorry."

Sometimes it's easiest just to come out with it.

"What did you say, Shane? Have you somethin in yer mouth?"

"Just a mint. She's dead, May."

"Dead is it? Are you sure? What happened, Shane?"

"Get another pet, May. A bigger one. One that can defend itself."

There was silence on the other end of the line. Was she praying silently to herself? Holding back tears? No, her voice was strong when she spoke again.

"Defend itself, is it? Against what, Shane? Evil?"

"I'll say no more for the moment. Be talkin to you, May. Sorry."

He heard her gulp. It was only sinking in now. Poor woman.

"I—I thought as much, Shane. I'd a feelin in me waters so I had. Thanks anyway."

You're welcome.

He put down the phone, gently.

❖

Shane estimated the crowd at the greyhound track to be four hundred, if not more. He looked at his card. Race Four. Dog No. 4. Dureen Flyer. Owner: Michael McCarthy. Her weight. Her previous form over the distance. The bookies were marking their boards and shouting the odds with such urgency you'd think there had been an earthquake or that a bomb had just gone off. It looked like dog No. 6 was the favourite at six to four. Dureen Flyer was second favourite at three to one. Her previous form looked promising enough, three times she had finished second and her time was improving as her track-craft got better. But last time out she was only fifth. She had been bumped at the first bend and again at the second and finished lame. All the other dogs were chalked up at four to one.

The dogs were on parade. Mick's black bitch had her head down, as if concentrating, indifferent to the crowd and to the bookies shouting their prices. No sign that her recent lameness had affected her. Seems to be a cross-section of society here. Young ones out for a night's fun. Others who know what the game is all about and had probably seen the ancestors of many of these greyhounds running in years gone by, winning, losing, injuring themselves, enthroned on high for their valiant feats or shot in the head for their failures.

Suddenly there was a ferocious flurry. Clutching a fat wad of notes, Mick had pounced. A chain reaction followed, others piling their money on. "Gimme four hundred on Dureen." It was all Dureen, Dureen, Dureen. Befuddled onlookers, ignorant of the impending coup, stared open-mouthed at the hullabaloo. A Japanese tourist looked around her in panic, caught up in the middle of a stampede.

Three to one was wiped off the boards. The No. 6 dog went out to two to one, then five to two. Mick's dog was seven to four. That only lasted a few seconds. Even money. Five to four on. With some bookies there were no offers available. Then the price was simply wiped off the board. Nothing left but a smudge of chalk. No more money was being taken on Dureen. The No. 6 dog drifted out to four to one. The other four dogs were now five to one, six to one or more. Nothing like it had been seen in years. A hush descended. Whatever the outcome, there would be talk about this operation long into the winter nights.

The bell rang. The electric hare shook itself and was quickly on the move.

❖

Back in Powl Duv, O'Dea's was bursting at the seams. If pubs were dying in rural Ireland then this looked like it could be the last stand or the beginning of the revival. The smoking ban and strict drinking and driving laws were just two pieces to the puzzling jigsaw of the demise. But tonight was like the old days all over again.

"Can't keep up with it," said Thady, a tray in each hand, "Mr McCarthy buying drinks all round. They're saying six bookies in Tralee cleaned out!"

Shane stood at the bar, nursing a hot whiskey, Mick at the other end of the counter, his back to him. A wasp was struggling to make its way along the counter. Late in the year for a wasp. Might be the last wasp in Powl Duv. The last wasp in Ireland? Insects. They, too, were part of a lost soundscape. Bees. Wasps. Shane studied the wasp's weary progress until it entered a little pool of spilt beer from which it frantically tried to escape. Then it gave up the ghost and drowned. Shane looked away and came into eye contact with Mick.

"Shane, you'll have one on me? Sure you will! Hey, Thady! Get that man—Thady, you're as deaf as a pole—get Shane what he's havin. And make it a large one!"

Shane declined with a polite nod of his head and emphasized again with a gesture of his hand that he was only in for the one. Thady looked at him and shrugged.

Mick extricated himself from his noisy hangers-on and lunged over to Shane.

"Go on! Have one on me. Made a bit of a killin earlier on tonight, so I did." He slapped Shane on the back, as if they were old drinking buddies.

"A killin is right. I know. I was there."

"You were at the track? Japers, Shane, didn't see you at all. Sure if I knew you had any bit of interest I would have let you in on it, d'ye know like, between ourselves." And he winked. It was hot in the bar and Shane had taken off his jacket and rolled up his shirt sleeves. Mick was looking at Shane's left arm.

"God, Shane, what war were you in? Them's a lot of scars. What's it goin to be, a hot whiskey?"

"Nothin, thanks... I was at the earlier killin too."

Mick's lip curled and his eyes glazed over.

"What do you mean?"

"I won't ask you how much you made tonight, Mick. None of my business. But May Kelly needs a new fridge."

"What the—? Are you sayin—? You're talkin riddles now, Shane," he said, clutching his glass like a weapon. Shane had to be careful. No point in antagonizing anyone, especially not the local postman cum historian cum gambling coup hero. Don't say too much now. Don't cause any rifts or vendettas in the community.

"Get her a new fridge, Mick, and nobody need know anything about the kitten. OK?"

Shane gave him his serious look. Deadly serious. The look that could bore its way through lies, hypocrisy, deceit and cant. A look that said, Do you want this all over the Kerry newspapers? On Radio Kerry? Do you want to keep your job as a postman?

Mick retreated a step or two.

"By God, aren't you the smart one," he hissed. "D'ya know what, you're after takin all the good out of the night, so you are. Anyway..." He seemed to change his tune, momentarily.

I think you're getting the message, Mick. Are you? Because I don't know how long more I can keep up with this bravado.

"I suppose I made more than enough on Dureen Flyer. If May needs a fridge she'll get one. Enjoy what's left of the night." He turned to go back to his cronies.

"Bella," said Shane.

"What?" said Mick, suddenly looking back as if stung in the neck by a wasp.

"That was the kitten's name."

From the PRIVATE DIARY of Shane O'Neil

The word *aingeal* means "angel". May was right. But it means more. More than that. A lot more. Trawling through the old dictionary has taught me that things are never as they appear. There are layers and layers of secondary, tertiary and hidden meanings, all waiting to be unearthed and handled with care and wonder.

> "*Aingeal*: an angel; a burnt-out cinder given in their hands as a protection to children going out at night."

It's all so strange. Heartbreakingly so. But kind of beautiful too. Doubly beautiful precisely because it reflects a vanished reality; only its primary meaning has remained intact. Yet, here it is before me, like a fly in amber, preserved for ever. Can we give some measure of life to it again, if only in the mind's eye? If it lives in the imagination, isn't that enough? What can live apart from the imagination? Can love exist if we fail to imagine it? Can hope exist?

> "*Meithiagán*: an insect that appears on or about 1st June."

Here we go again. What size is this thing? What colour? Nothing. It's all so cryptic. I wouldn't know one if I saw one. I have a feeling it might be red. I don't know why.

> "*Sagairtín*: a little priest; an inedible periwinkle."

Holy smoke!

> "*Buarach bháis*: an unbroken hoop of skin cut with incantation from a corpse across the entire body from shoulder to foot sole and wrapped in silk of the colours of the rainbow and used as

a spancel to tie the legs of a person to produce certain effects by witchcraft."

Don't know what to say. Beyond me, way beyond me.

"*Donn*: a prince, a chief, a judge; the name of a fairy inhabiting sandbanks off the Clare coast."

Where exactly are these sandbanks? Do they still exist?

"*Sleith*: carnal intercourse with a woman, without her consent or knowledge."

Without her knowledge?

"*Iarmhaireacht*: loneliness felt at cock-crow."

This could lead to madness.

❖

If I say the words over and over again, will they form part of my mental furniture? It wouldn't do to mix them up, to confuse the *meithiagán* with the *sagairtín*. But does anyone know these words any more? Does anyone care? This is no way to learn a language. Must buy a CD or two. Tomorrow. Without fail.

❖

Took a walk earlier on today. Didn't see a soul. Leaves rolled and tumbled along the road towards me, sometimes crossing the road without looking: like children at play, or fleeing some terror?

Can I exist here, on my own? Won't it become lonely or monotonous? Why can't life be like one of those old Dutch or Flemish paintings, with people enjoying themselves and each other's company, out in the open, or in taverns, celebrating different seasons, significant or insignificant events in their lives with vigour and gusto. I want to celebrate these scurrying leaves, yellow, greenish-brown, russet, some turning black. But with whom? How?

❖

Listened to a flamenco concert on the radio. Imagined Róisín as the dancer. Yes, that's her name. A little rose. Róisín! (Who's been doing some detective work lately? KDA all the way!)

Saw her in robes of orange, the oranges of Seville, orange of the rising sun. Castanets. My beating heart. The cry of the gypsy singer.

She stomps. Stomps on a thousand reports. With fury. She laughs as she stomps. Grinds them into the ground. Sending them off to hell. My reports. My useless reports. My waste of ink. Wasted life. The flamenco singer cries. She responds to him. He roars, almost. The voice breaks at times. As though the heart inside is breaking. It cracks open. The heart. Blood pours out. The Roma blood of centuries. Centuries of love and hate. Centuries of wandering. The wandering heart. The wandering soul. Wandering fool. Wandering sage. Wandering minstrel.

Too many reports. Words are swimming, spinning out of control.

—Dutch Diaries (destroyed) of Shane O'Neil

Chapter 6

Something in the Air

Shane found himself in Tralee one day, looking for a book. Any book. A long book. To go with the long evenings. He browsed in one section after another. *Under the Greenwood Tree* by Thomas Hardy. He liked the title. Opening it, he began to read:

> To dwellers in a wood, almost every species of tree has its voice as well as its feature. At the passing of the breeze, the fir-trees sob and moan no less distinctly than they rock; the holly whistles as it battles with itself; the ash hisses amid its quiverings; the beech rustles while its flat boughs rise and fall...

Shane read it over and over again, savouring the rhythm of the prose. He hadn't come across anything like it before. The more he read it the more astonished he became. Was the author making it all up? Or could it be true? Every word? Do fir trees sob? Would he ever come to know a wood in this way? Dureen Wood. What kind of trees are they? What species? Shane didn't know.

"Can I help you?"

Shane jumped, dropping the book that was in his hand.

"Didn't mean to startle you!"

The shop assistant looked like a temp, a student perhaps. He stooped to pick up the book, glanced at the title and deftly handed it back to Shane, as if it were the type of thing he did every day.

"Any other books by Hardy?"

"Afraid not. There's a book about Laurel and Hardy though."

Should I laugh, thought Shane. Was that a joke? And why do people say "I'm afraid", when they don't mean it?

Shane didn't know what he was looking for. What was the name of the local publisher? Bee's Knees? No. Pyjamas! The Cat's Pyjamas.

"What titles have you from the local publisher? The Cat's Pyjamas."

The assistant looked around. Was he some kind of a dancer? He performed what could only be described as a balletic twirl. Shane got the distinct feeling that the young man was on the lookout and didn't want to be overheard.

"Nothing, I'm afraid."

I'm afraid again, thought Shane. But he didn't look afraid. Not in the least bit.

"What? All sold out?"

"Don't do business with them anymore. Any particular book you were looking for?"

"A good long read."

"*The Book of Cocks.*"

"I beg your pardon?"

"Ha ha! Everyone reacts like that."

It was an anthology, four hundred pages or more. Poems from around the world. About cockerels.

Who comes up with these mad ideas for books?

Shane opened a page, idly. A Slovenian poet, Milan Dekleva, had written:

> A rooster, spy of the light, has taken my head away
> And bequeathed it to the river...

"No, I was thinking more of—" Shane was distracted by the shop assistant's movements. Gyrations, moving his body to the rhythm of some background music. An Abba song.

No, this is not what I'm looking for.

Why didn't they stock the local publisher's titles? Some little local war about nothing. Mysterious.

"If I can be of any help at all. Humour? Gardening? Soccer? Section over there is quite popular. Detective novels from Scandinavia. Buy two, get the third one free."

"Really?" Shane walked over and examined one of the books. It had over three hundred pages. That would get him through a few long, murky evenings. Two novels and a third one free. He could take some notes, combining research with pleasure. Hold on a minute. Notes? You don't want to start writing reports again. No bloody way.

"Any Dutch detective novels?"

"Dutch? No. At least, don't think so. Not full-time here."

Will I tell him? Yeah. Why not.

"I'm a detective myself."

The assistant looked at him intently, disbelievingly at first.

"You're not the man out in Powl Duv by any chance?"

"That's me." Shane attempted a little smirk. "News travels fast."

"Strange place, Powl Duv." The assistant's mood had suddenly become cloudy.

"In what way?" asked Shane, noticing the change, his brief moment of happiness at being recognized had gone.

"Know the sign that says population 35?"

"36 actually."

"36? Really? 36? Plot thickens."

"What do you mean?"

The assistant turned away and ran a finger along a row of books, as if looking for dust. He hummed a bit of the Abba song. His back was to Shane when he said, "Where are they all?" He turned around in a manner that suggested he might have been an amateur actor in his spare time and peered at Shane, repeating the question, a little spookily.

Shane backed away, still clutching a Scandinavian tome.

"I don't know. How should I know?"

"You're the gumshoe."

"Didn't think they use that word around here."

"They don't. Speaking of words. They say 'tay' out there instead of 'tea'."

"What's wrong with that?"

"Sure that's Elizabethan! Living in some kind of a time-warp they are."

"Would you prefer if they spoke like Americans?"

The assistant took the detective book from Shane as one might take a dangerous toy from a child and replaced it on the shelf.

"We'll forget about that book, shall we? Be like a busman's holiday. Why would you be reading about your own line of work? Where's the escape in that? Not that there isn't more to reading than escapism. Can I recommend something? Something meaty?"

"Meaty?" What did he mean? Shane looked at him suspiciously.

The assistant laughed. "Did you think I meant under the counter stuff? None of that. *The Book of Cocks* is the closest we have to that! Something to chew on is what I meant."

"To chew on? I don't know. Maybe. What kind of book is it?"

Shane felt he was being lead down a garden path.

"You'll love it or hate it. *The Book of Disquiet* by Fernando something-or-other. Ever hear of him?"

"Who? Afraid not." Shane was conscious of having used the afraid word. And it made him slightly afraid. The conversation was beginning to make him feel spooked.

"You'll be completely and utterly sane after it, or so I'm told, or it'll drive you bananas entirely." The assistant began to giggle. The upper part of his body wanted to spring away from the rest of him. Was the man insane? And the song in the background hadn't changed. It was in a loop, repeating itself.

"I just came in for—I, I don't know exactly what I was looking for. Maybe I'll know it when I see it." Shane turned to the nearest shelf.

"This one here? *The Battle of Kinsale*. My ancestors fought... Hello?" The assistant had disappeared. There was an eerie silence for a minute or two. Shane felt alone, alone in the shop, alone in the universe. He tried to read a page from *The Battle of Kinsale*: "O'Neill's submission meant the end of the native chieftains. The consequences would be catastrophic. Gaelic Ireland began to disintegrate..."

"Voilà!" Shane jumped.

"Beg your pardon. Did I startle you? I do that all the time. Manager calls me the Mexican Jumping Bean. Won't let me near his dogs. Here it is. *The Book of Disquiet.* Highly recommended." The assistant grinned. As the grin scarcely lasted a few seconds, Shane couldn't figure out was it a menacing or a friendly grin. The assistant held the book out to him, as though offering a chocolate or a drink. What was he to do. Refuse?

He took it, handling it gingerly, like some exotic fruit. *The Book of Disquiet.* He didn't like the title very much.

"Fernando Pessoa? Never heard of him. Spanish, is he? The Spanish weren't much help to us at Kinsale, were they?"

"Not Spanish. Portuguese."

"Fiction?"

"Good question."

What's going on? Good question! You're beginning to annoy me.

"You mean you haven't read it?"

"God, no. Only trying to sell it because of a bet."

Shane looked at the back cover, his thoughts on the assistant: is he trying to make a fool of me, or what? Such were his suspicions that his eyes had travelled to the end of the blurb without taking in one word.

"Bet? What exactly do you mean?" Shane was losing patience.

"With the manager. He says I won't be able to sell it for love or money."

"Where's the manager?" asked Shane.

"Out walking the dogs. Greyhounds. I just fill in for him when he's out. Five euros an hour. Not much is it? Spends more money on his dogs than on me. Five euros an hour is plenty for a young lad like me, says he; it's educating myself I should be and reading a couple of books a day. Polish my mind. Won't be polishing it with Mr Pessoa here, that's for sure. Hope someone buys it, though. Stand to win twenty euros."

"Buy it yourself and claim the twenty euros!"

"Never thought of that."

How come?

"Do you read much yourself?"

"Bit of local history."

"What are you reading at the moment?"

"Book about William Melville."

Who? The name meant nothing to Shane.

"From Direenaclaurig Cross."

Where?

"Direen—?

"Direenaclaurig Cross. In Sneem. Not too far away. About 50 miles."

"What's his claim to fame?"

Let me guess... hmmm, no idea.

"Head of British Secret Service. Codename 'M.' Ring a bell? James Bond?"

"Really?"

A bit far-fetched.

"Wouldn't be admired by everyone around here. Know what I mean?"

"Because?"

"Tortured a lot of Fenians. Bit of a traitor. Ever hear of the Jubilee Plot?"

"Remind me."

"British Government plot to assassinate Queen Victoria. Blame it on the Fenians."

The clipped manner of his speech suggested subterfuge. A Fenian on the run. Had the book about this Melville character he was reading caused his imagination to run riot?

"William Melville, you say?"

The assistant nodded.

"Learn something every day," Shane conceded. "Is there a shop around here where I can buy some mints?"

"Mints? Four doors up."

◆

Shane paused for a moment at the door. It was decorated with a map of medieval Ireland showing major battle sites. Major? He had never heard of most of them:

Clontarf 1014

Dublin 1171

Downpatrick 1260

Callann 1261

Dysert O'Dea 1318

Faughert 1318

Pilltown 1462

Knockdoe 1504

Dublin—(again!)—1534

Farsetmore 1567

Clontibret 1595

Yellow Ford 1598

Moyry Pass 1600

Kinsale 1601

Those people outside, walking the footpaths, crossing the street, in their cars, on bicycles, at the hairdressers, saying a prayer in a church, their ancestors had fought in battles, here in Ireland, or as mercenaries in some foreign war, the Thirty Years War, the American Civil War, the Irish Civil War, the Spanish Civil War, the First World War, the Second World War, or in ancient unrecorded battles, the air freezing with their battle cries, the earth groaning under the weight of the dead.

The Great O'Neill had won at Yellow Ford. That much he knew. When will war be made illegal and armies unnecessary?

"How much is the map?" he asked, warily, half-expecting the assistant to spring out of nowhere, maybe with a battle-axe.

"Sorry. Not for sale," came the disembodied voice that segued into the Abba song: "There was something in the air that night, the stars shone bright, Fernando..."

85

Shane heard the ring of the till. The assistant must have taken his advice and bought the book.

Are my eyes as dull as they feel?

One of these days they will fall out of my head, hop off the desk,

roll down the corridor, out on to the street and be eaten by a sick

cat.

—Dutch Diaries (destroyed) of Shane O'Neil

Chapter 7

Sláinte!

Weeks and months went trundling by and one morning winter decided to visit Powl Duv. Not a winter to imprison one in ice—as had reputedly happened to Shane's ancestors—but a winter, at least in name, and bare trees to prove it. Dureen Wood was denuded of its mystery. Hardly a wood at all now, some eighty or more stands— yet its presence was more pronounced than ever.

Will I still be here on the first of June, he thought? Will I recognize it, the *meithiagán*. I wonder what it's like? A little red speck running about on... how many legs? How is it distinguished from other insects? How fast does it move? Is it a pest?

Thinking back, he couldn't remember having seen any insects in The Hague. Not one. But I must have, he thought, and if he had spotted himself just then in a mirror his look of incredulity would have astounded him.

Shane had settled into a routine. O'Dea's Famous Stew was all right once a month or so, but he needed to be more self-reliant and had bought himself a no-nonsense cookbook by a British celebrity chef on his second visit to the bookshop in Tralee. He had specifically asked for an Irish cookbook but the British celebrity chef was all they had. After a while it hit him that none of the ingredients for some of the more tempting recipes were available locally—asparagus, shitake mushrooms, monkfish. And so, he found himself going to Tralee more often than he originally intended. On one of these pilgrimages he bumped into Róisín

O'Connor, the bangharda who had previously made an impression when she called to his house with her surly sergeant. He didn't recognize her at first. She wasn't in uniform.

"Been shoppin then, Mr O'Neil?"

She has such a bold, confident manner about her. No place for a shrinking violet in the police force, I suppose.

"Mints and stuff."

"Mints?"

She grinned.

Offer her one, you cretin!

"You'll be gettin the four o'clock bus back to Powl Duv?"

"Correct," said Shane. How clipped, how terse his sentences had become over the years. How impersonal.

"Care for a coffee or something?" he asked.

"Yeah, or somethin. I'm off duty so you can offer me somethin a bit stronger if you like. Róisín, by the way. Róisín O'Connor."

He didn't know should they shake hands or not. Had the continental kiss on the cheek—or both cheeks and then a third time—come to Tralee yet? Well, if it has you've missed the opportunity, he thought. No, a kiss on the cheek wasn't going to happen. Bit early for that. Far too early. What are you thinking?

He extended his hand.

"Shane."

She laughed. "I know who you are! Wasn't I up at your house!"

I'd like to kick myself, kick myself all the way back to Powl Duv. To The Hague. No. No. Not going back there. Never.

He had held her hand too long. She took it back.

"Where would you recommend, Róisín?"

Am I saying her name correctly? Where's the emphasis, first or second syllable? Does it matter? Yes, of course it matters. Everything matters!

"Anywhere really. It doesn't matter. One place is almost as good as the next. It's important to spread your custom around you know."

Shane looked up and down the street. They were spoilt for choice. The nearest pub was a mere fifty yards away.

"Let's try Moriarty's, so," she said, breezily. "Sure it's as good as the next."

"Fair enough. Bit of a nip in the air. Hot whiskey?"

"Grand!" she said.

There were no more than five customers in the bar. All eyes looked up as they entered.

Shane ordered two hot whiskies. She glanced at his shopping bags.

"Cookin for yourself, I suppose?" Her voice betrayed some concern. Was it pity? Compassion? Pity, he thought. But ever so slight. Whatever she was thinking, her eyes remained bright, dark blue eyes that shone like pools in a sun shower.

"*Sláinte!*" They clicked glasses. He swirled the whiskey around in the glass and gently sipped it. He counted the cloves that were stuck to the slice of lemon. Four. Like four bullet points in one of his summaries. An unfortunate habit, counting. Habit of a lifetime. Noticing every detail in the hope that the jigsaw might fit together somehow, or throw up an unexpected clue. Not in real life, of course. In the reports. Looking for inconsistencies. I mean, that's all it was, correct? Nothing more than that. If three was mentioned on page 24, three of anything, it doesn't matter, and suddenly it's four on page 46, that's what he had to spot, wasn't it? Computers were doing it now. Good for them. Now he was free to spot other things. Things computers can't spot. A moist lip. Bright things. Glistening things. Did she have a ring on her finger? No, Róisín was ringless.

Where do we go from here? His mouth craved a mint. Is there someone else? No, you don't ask that. Maybe when you are in a relationship. Not before. What is it? What is the question? Do you have a boyfriend? No. Start with brothers and sisters. Then move on to... she wouldn't have joined him for a drink if she had a steady boyfriend. Would she? Maybe she's—perish the thought. That's my problem. I can't kill thoughts. Maybe the sergeant sent her to spy on me? Why can't I kill thoughts? Do they have a life of their own? Let's say I have a thought, in embryo, the beginning of a thought, a spark, an idea, and let's say I have a stroke, or go into a coma, or die... does the thought continue to form, to express itself, to make itself known as a fully fledged thought? Has a thought a life of its own?

"Penny for your thoughts!"

Her voice came from some muffled zone, some unimagined galaxy. He looked at her.

"Isn't it funny we still say penny? Nobody says a cent for your thoughts."

"Hmmm... yes, funny," she said. Shane could see she wasn't a bit impressed by his observation.

Not a bit funny.

She was smaller than he, perhaps only five foot six inches, but seemed perfectly proportioned. I thought you had to be a certain height to get into the guards? Shane found himself repeating the words "perfectly proportioned" and began to feel increasingly annoyed with himself. Why couldn't he just say pretty? Or gorgeous. Because that's what she was. In or out of uniform, Róisín O'Connor was gorgeous.

You're gorgeous. "Absolutely g—"

"What?"

"Nothin."

He felt his gorge rising.

"Were you tryin to say somethin to me, Shane O'Neil?"

"Sorry, Róisín. I—"

"You what, you fool, ya?" She laughed. Her teeth shone.

Fool? Sweet suffering Jesus, don't turn into a Sphinx!

He had been called a fool before. Now, for the first time, it sounded sweet, unbearably sweet.

She looked again at his shopping bags.

"Oh, nothing very exciting there, I'm afraid. Turnips. Potatoes. Smoked haddock. Simple country fare. Can't go wrong there, I suppose. Hard to overcook a turnip. Or so I'm told."

"You've no one to cook for you? I mean—wouldn't you get someone—someone to come in and do a bit of cleanin or ironin or cookin for you or stuff like that?"

"I'm thinkin of it. There's May, May Kelly do you know her?"

"Kind of..."

"She does a bit of B & B in the summer but has nothing much to do for the rest of the year. Do you think I should ask her?"

She quaffed down her whiskey.

"Nothin to lose?"

"You'll have another?"

"My twist!" She winked at the barman, indicating the same again.

She didn't have to attract his attention. He was watching the pair, closely. Róisín O'Connor, having a drink with yer man from the KDA—the Kerry Detective Agency, mind you. What a story! It would keep him going all night with the customers. All night? All week.

"Nice place," said Shane, looking around. "Come here often?"

Róisín did not disguise her disappointment. Of course she was disappointed. What kind of a question is that? Do you come here often? Shane felt like making his excuses and absconding before he had painted himself into a corner.

"Now, Róisín!" The bar boy beamed. "Two hot whiskies—for the hottest girl in Kerry."

"Watch yerself, boyo. What do I owe you?"

"On the house, Róisín." The bar boy grinned.

"Good man yourself. I'll go easy on you next time I see you speedin in that rickety old Cortina of yours! It must be twice as old as yourself."

Shane made one last effort to communicate sanely, sculpting a smile on lips that were on the brink of trembling.

"On the house?"

"One of the perks of the trade," she said. "*Sláinte an bhradáin!*" Guessing he might not have known what she had just said, she translated: "Health of the salmon!"

"Oh! Haven't got as far as that yet."

"You're learnin Irish? That's great."

"Would you like a mint?" He reached for the shopping bag. "I've two sorts here. One with a hole."

He intended it to sound funny. Now as he fumbled with the mints he thought that it might have sounded like some juvenile double entendre.

Lecherous. Sleazy. Vulgar. What kind of a—I'm some kind of a Neanderthal, am I? Talking about turnips. What next? Am I going to start blabbering about the weather?

"Think it's going to rain?"

Now I've done it. I shouldn't be let out.

"Are you goin to give me one of those mints or not?" said Róisín, in mock exasperation.

"Oh, sure. Sorry."

"Not cold enough for rain, Shane."

"That rhymes!" he said. And as soon as he said it he thought to himself, yeah, Shane, it also rhymes with pain. If only he could switch off. He sensed that she was now making conversation just for the sake of it. But he wasn't sure.

It's natural to talk about the weather. May Kelly talks about the weather. Every day.

"A few years in Kerry and you'll be able to smell the rain. Oh, you'll smell it all right, well before it starts raining on the Blaskets."

"Will I? Do you think I will? That could turn out to be useful, I'm sure."

He became conscious of the fact that she had just called him by his name. The sound of his own name, on her lips, touched him like a lazy summer tide lapping at a boulder.

"You never know. Anyway, tell me, how's business?"

"Business? I'm not really in business, Róisín. Retired. The Kerry Detective Agency is just, well, something to do, but only if something comes my way. If nothing turns up well and good, if not it's all the same to me. I'm not touting for business if you know what I mean. If there's nothing going on I can go fishing."

She looked at him.

"Do you fish?"

"No." He looked down at his shoes. He didn't fish, didn't play golf. It dawned on him that he had no hobby, no sport. Reading. Listening to relaxing music. Do they count? But the KDA was meant to be a pastime. Wasn't it? A hobby. Something to do.

94

"You're too young to be retired, so you are." She looked away and her eyes darted this way and that, making sure she wasn't being overheard by anyone else.

"I could put some business in your way if you like."

She said it in a hushed tone.

"You could? What kind of business?" Shane felt his eyebrows were ever so slightly raised. What had happened to his poker face?

"Business! Your kind of business. It's not in the business of knittin woolly jumpers we are, is it?"

They both laughed and looked at each other, enjoying each other's mirth, briefly.

Thank God she's laughing. Don't stop!

"I don't think the sergeant would like it very much if you put a few cold cases my way."

She sensed that Shane didn't like the sergeant very much.

"You don't like him? Nobody does! His own worst enemy."

"He's got sanpaku eyes!"

"What in the name of God is that?"

"You now when a baby is born, the eye is kind of full. No white above or below."

"Right, I follow you. Go on."

"Well. First, let me tell you how I know about this. I got it from a Mr Takiguchi, Japanese prison warden. He was visiting Europol. Most boring man on earth. I didn't think so. But my bosses did. So Muggins here was the one who had to bring him out for lunch. When the waiter had taken our order, Mr Takiguchi says, "Very sick man! Eating too much meat, salt, salami, hard cheeses!" And then he told me all about the sanpaku thing. If the whites show under your eyes you are yin sanpaku. You are not in a healthy state. Nervous system is impaired. If the whites show above your eye, you are what's called yang sanpaku. A violent, dangerous person. A Charles Manson. The sergeant is yang sanpaku!"

"Holy Mother of God, he's not is he? I must write that word down. How do you spell it?"

Róisín was between shock and amusement.

"S-a-n-p-a-k-u. Please don't tell him I said that."

She scribbled the word on a beer mat and popped it into her jacket pocket.

"I won't breathe a word," Róisín assured him. "But now that you mention it, I've seen that look on him. I've seen the whites in his eyes. Many's the time. Scary. He can be violent, too, betimes, so he can. That's true. And he's always stuffin himself with cheeseburgers and lashins of salty fries."

"Well, there you go!"

Shane looked away and she saw that he had fixed his gaze momentarily on the clock.

"Got to catch that bus. We'll talk again."

"Please God," she said.

Why the bus all of a sudden? What's the rush? You could have got a taxi. There's bound to be a hackney service. Am I running away?

She leaned forward. He could feel her warm breath.

"I'm not sanpaku, am I?"

Shane looked into her eyes. He could have gazed there for an eternity.

"Not a bit!"

She laughed. "Neither are you, Shane O'Neil."

They both knocked back the remainder of the whiskey and went to the door.

She turned round, smiled and waved to the barman. He winked back at her.

❖

He took the last seat on the bus and placed the shopping bag on the vacant seat next to him. He thought of the encounter with Róisín, all the things he hadn't asked her about: the list morphed into a bizarre interrogation session in his mind, interfering with the initial pleasure of his thoughts. He was evaluating her. Evaluating himself. How truthful had he been? How evasive? How would he evaluate himself? Come on now. Honestly. As a human being. Efficient? Trustworthy. Yes. But, let's admit it, a shade dull. But now, as the bus lurched into the dusk, he was enveloped by a glow that was far from dull. He dismissed the idea before it had time to fully form itself. Glow? Nothing more than the effect of two ten year-old whiskies. He had misinterpreted her signals. Maybe there were no signals. She was just being friendly. To a stranger. That's all. Nothing more. Think of the age difference. She's at least twenty years younger. More?

He looked out. As though searching high and low for the last glimmers of light, starlings riddled the sky.

"Aren't you getting off here? Hey, yourself there in the back! O'Neil, isn't it? Powl Duv!"

The bus driver had awoken him from his reverie. Shane reprimanded himself.

Detectives are not supposed to be dreamy. They should be wide awake and have some clue as to where they live. Darkness had already spread its first layer over the village and the evening star twinkled like a silver coin, a coin he had tossed high up in the air and far into his dreams.

It took him the best part of half an hour to prepare dinner. The end result was pedestrian enough. Would May Kelly have made a better job of it? Or Róisín O'Connor? These days women had better things to do.

From the PRIVATE DIARY of Shane O'Neil

Heard some yodelling on the radio. Mesmerized. Could hardly believe my ears. Something else. Totally. Like colonic irrigation, not of the stomach but of the ears. I thought Gypsy and Flamenco music did something for me. But yodelling is another kettle of fish.

Something snapped in me. The yodelling did it, like a high note that can crack glass. Crack! Something that had long lain frozen. What was it? Why was I stuck behind a desk in Holland? Why didn't I learn something useful? Wouldn't it be great to be able to yodel? If I could yodel, I feel I could fly out of myself. Like a mountain lark. Up into the thin, yodelling air. There's such a strange purity about it. What is it really saying, I wonder?

It's also slightly comic. I need the comic. More than the tears of Gypsies. What are the chances of learning how to yodel in Ireland, I wonder? In Tralee? Slim. Though, you never know, do you? I'll put a small ad in the *Kerryman*. Wanted: Yodelling Classes. You never know.

Then again, maybe it's too late to be thinking about anything like that. Build up the detective agency. KDA. Don't get sidelined. Yodelling? What were you thinking? And anyway, to go all the way with it, you'd have to wear lederhosen and stick a feather in your hat. Next thing you know you're a Neo-Nazi. How's the Kerry Detective Agency going to stand over that? A yodelling detective? No. Impossible.

Good night, Diary. Good night, Róisín. Gypsies and yodellers everywhere, good night to you all.

If you are reading this you are doing so without my permission.

Pokkelijder!

—Dutch Diaries (destroyed) of Shane O'Neil

Chapter 8

My Head is Missing

Was it thunderous rain? No. A fierce rapping on the door.
"Shane! Come quick! My head is missin!"

He fell out of the bed. It was May's voice.

Her head is missing? What could that mean?

He dressed hurriedly, rinsed out his mouth and rushed out the door. Unshaven, exposed to a raw morning wind, he felt foolish, scattered.

Doggedly, head down, he trudged the short distance to Cooleen.

"He was stolen before, you know," said May, handing him a cup of tea.

"Who, what are you talk—?"

"The god!"

Shane's head reeled.

"God? What god?"

"Ah, Shane, what is it you think I'm talkin about?"

"I've no idea," exclaimed Shane. Then he thought of sitting down, finally.

"Duán, a curse on him. The ould god. His head's been stolen—again!"

I'm out of my depth here.

"It's over ten years ago since the last time he disappeared. Came back again, mysteriously, after a fortnight. Wait until I get some more milk out of the fridge."

"New fridge, May?"

"No, no. Why do you ask?"

"I thought it died on you."

"Who told you that?"

"You did."

"Well, it did. But do you know what? Didn't Mick the Posht fix it for me."

"He did, did he? Oh."

He looked at May. He remembered Róisín. The way he had looked at her. With the beginning of desire. Róisín, what are you, who are you? Are you a genie, a fairy, a vision or a wisp? And when he realized what was happening, that he was staring at May and imagining Róisín, his desire cooled instantly. What was it anyway, this desire, but the desire of the human race to perpetuate itself, to repeat the same mistakes over and over again and to die. To go on like that. Forever. Or until the mystery of it all might be solved.

"*In saecula saeculorum,*" he intoned and May looked at him queerly.

"I'll get the clippings," she said.

Shane sipped his tea, wondering was he fully awake. Clippings? What clippings? Toe-nail clippings? When a woman like May, living alone, gets too old and stiff to cut her own toenails, does someone come along and clip them for her?

She plonked a folder on his lap, loosely filled with newspaper clippings.

"Read all about it! I've some clothes to put out on the line."

The articles described the disappearance of an ancient Celtic artefact, a stone head of the god Duán. Experts from the National Museum of Ireland were quoted as saying that it was one of the oldest artefacts of its type in existence. "Much battered by the elements," he read, "it is clearly a head but the face is almost featureless. Time has worn most of the details away but there is evidence that erosion was also caused by ritual rubbing, possibly people in search of a cure. The ears, eyes and nose are almost gone but the mouth still wears an inscrutable grin."

May came back in.

"What do you think of it all then, Shane?"

"Beats me," was all Shane could muster.

She strode over to the window and dusted the VACANCIES sign without touching the fly that was crawling on it, indifferent to her dusting. A pet fly?

"They'll be back now in their droves. Reporters. Photographers. Museum people. And the odd nutcase. I'll have to get in a big supply of bacon, eggs and tomatoes. Do you like tomatoes? I don't know what people see in them. Now, what else? Maybe I'll make a list. Mushrooms..." She no longer noticed he was there. He slipped out quietly.

There was an envelope on the floor when Shane got back. No name on it. No stamp. He sat down before opening it.

"What in the—?" exclaimed Shane. It appeared to be in Greek. What was is? A poem? He stared at it for a long time:

Έκοψα το κεφάλι μου
το 'βαλα σ' ένα πιάτο
και το πήγα στο γιατρό μου

—Δεν έχει τίποτε, μου είπε,
είναι απλώς πυρακτωμένο
ρίξε το μέσα στο ποτάμι και θα ιδούμε

το 'ριξα στο ποτάμι μαζί με τους βατράχους
τότε είναι που χάλασε τον κόσμο
άρχισε κάτι παράξενα τραγούδια
να τρίζει φοβερά και να ουρλιάζει

το πήρα και το φόρεσα πάλι στο λαιμό μου

γύριζα έξαλλος τους δρόμους

με πράσινο εξαγωνομετρικό κεφάλι ποιητή

Chapter 9

The Red Hand

The doorbell rang.

"Mr O'Neil?"

"Yes?"

"Can I come in?"

He was a smallish fellow with glasses, wearing a blue pullover, as blue as a forget-me-not, and his blue eyes darted this way and that, unsettlingly, as though trying to notice different things at the same time.

"Of course."

"I haven't had the pleasure. Tommy Ashe. The *Kerryman*. Lovely office you have. You should see the state of—can I sit down?"

"Do, please. Can I offer you some tea, coffee?"

Tommy declined.

"I'll tell you why I'm here. I'm trying to get a vox pop from the locals, you know, about the missing head, like. I was wondering have you any theories or anything at all you'd like to share with our readers?"

"I'm not working on the case if that's what you mean," blurted Shane, noticing that his visitor had blue stockings. Shane couldn't say why, but the blue stockings unnerved him slightly.

"No, Shane, if I can call you that. I wasn't implying—do you mind if we tape this? I see you have a turf fire. A lovely thing it is too. Be sure not to burn any wood from Dureen. Strange wood that. Wicked stuff. Doesn't burn proper at all, I'm told. Funny old smell off it too. Right,

105

I'll switch this on, so. Do you know, it's the way I can't read my own shorthand most of the time."

"I've really very little to say on the matter," said Shane hoping to be relieved of this nuisance sooner rather than later.

"Ah sure, nobody had all that much to say the last time either. But times have changed. People aren't as tight-lipped as they used to be. It's a more liberal society now, isn't it? It is surely. People can say anything they like now. You can't shut them up. Everybody has opinions about everything now. I suppose they're more informed. Whatever they have to say, we'll print it—if it's in everybody's best interests. Know what I mean?"

Shouldn't have let you in. Should have given some excuse.

"But what can I tell you?" pleaded Shane.

"Should the head have been allowed to be in Powl Duv in the first place?"

"What do you mean?"

What do I know about the head?

Shane was slightly intrigued by the line of questioning but part of him found the whole business too strange to contemplate.

"There are them that say it should never have been allowed to be here in the first place. It's in a museum it should be. In Tralee. Or up in Dublin."

"I never heard of the head until today."

"Go away! I thought everyone knew about it. Goes to show. You've heard of the poet who's resting over in Dureen Wood?"

"He's been mentioned."

"If he'll ever rest, poor man... But you haven't heard of him in connection with the head?"

"No."

"A quare one that is. No, you say? Well, it doesn't matter."

Shane didn't like false trails or bits of information leading nowhere. His curiosity was aroused.

"No, I'd love to know. What's the connection? Tell me."

"Ah, it's just part of the folklore. Not much interested in it myself. Heard the granny talkin about it once or twice, so I did."

"Go on."

"I'll just switch off the tape for a minute."

"OK."

Tommy Ashe wiggled his jawbone, pursed his lips and looked over his shoulder several times before commencing. Was this for some kind of dramatic effect or did he really want to make sure he wasn't being overheard? Shane forced himself to smile, encouragingly. Tommy lowered his voice.

"Women who were unable to conceive. They'd go up there to Cooleen, where May's house is now, where the head is—or was—on designated moonlit nights. The poet would be there to greet the woman. Are you with me? He'd put a hand on her belly—like this, look—and the other hand on the head—Duán's head—and then he'd do his muttering. Like this. Can I show you?"

Don't touch me.

"No need, Tommy. I can imagine it. Go on. What kind of muttering?"

"Muttering."

"And she'd have to drink buttermilk and all the while the poet would be muttering his old fertility charm."

"Do you know it?"

"The charm? I have it. I do. I heard my grandmother saying it, oh yes, yes, many's the time. She'd keep us entertained with them old stories and pishogues when we were in short pants. How did it go again?

> *Bláthach bhán fé sholas na gealaí*
> *Leanbh geal in áras do chléibh i gceann naoi mí*

That was it."

Shane felt a little queasy. Tommy's voice had changed as he uttered the charm, it was as if someone else was speaking—his grandmother, maybe—and he himself a mere medium.

"What does it mean?"

"Yerra, some old nonsense about buttermilk, dancing under the moonlight and conceiving a baby. I'll put the tape on again if you don't mind. OK, one, two, three and—rolling."

"And did it work? The charm?"

"Nine times out of ten," came the swift reply. "Anyway, what our readers would like to know is this. You're a sophisticated kind of man now, Shane, by all accounts. You've been around the block, as they say."

"A few times. For my sins."

"Knowing what you know now about the missing head, wouldn't you say we're better off without all that pagan carry-on?"

"I really don't know."

"How d'ya mean you don't know?"

"I don't know." What part of "I don't know" don't you understand?

"Ah, come on now, Shane."

"If something is part of your history, local history, it belongs in the landscape, doesn't it? Not in a museum. I suppose things are safer in a museum but, I don't know, they're better in the local environment. If possible. I don't know. I haven't thought about it much."

"Good. I like it. A quote at last! I can use that," and Tommy Ashe grinned, his first proper grin of the day.

"History is history after all," mused Shane, getting into the spirit of things, his gaze being carried out towards the hordes of dark clouds intent on conquering the skies over Powl Duv.

"Keep going, Shane, this is good. This is the kind of stuff we want." Tommy's eyes twinkled.

"The pagan past. The Celtic past. The Christian past. Vikings. Normans. English. East Europeans. It's all part of the endless weave, isn't it?"

"God, I think we have it now—'All Part of the Weave says Local Detective'! We'll leave the East Europeans out of it. Too recent. We'll keep it nice and ancient, if we can."

"Well look, I'm no expert... Tommy, isn't it? And anyway..."

"You know as much as the next man. Maybe more. Don't worry. It'll be grand. Honest to God. You don't mind if I take a photo? Don't stir. Just as you are."

"I've been thinking. Can I hold up my left hand, like this?"

"You can do anything you like, Shane. You're in your own house."

"The hand doesn't look funny?"

"No, it's—what can I tell you? Unusual to say the least. Hold it, steady! Here we go. One more. And another. Grand!"

"I can put down the hand?"

"You can, Shane. What's the crack with the hand, if you don't mind me askin?"

"Well, it came into my head just now and I'd like if you could put it into the paper. The old gods aren't as far away as some people would like us to believe."

"Keep going, Shane. Love it. Taking it all down."

"The Ó Néill symbol is the Lámh Dhearg, the Red Hand."

"Oh yeah, the Lámh Dhearg. We were told something about that in school."

"Well now, I don't know what you were taught, but the sun god in pagan times, he had a red hand. And that's where the Ó Néill clan got it from."

"Fantastic, Shane. Brilliant! God, this is more than I was expecting! Amazing!"

He got up to go.

"May I show you something?"

"Of course."

Shane handed him the page of Greek.

"Any idea what it might be?"

Tommy looked at the page and looked up at Shane, wide-eyed.

"Russian, is it?" he asked.

"Greek. It came in the door, unmarked envelope."

"He's at it again, so."

"Who?"

"Dunno. A prankster. He has half of North Kerry demented. Women are goin out of their minds. They don't know if its salacious or obscene or threatening or what it is because it's always in some foreign language. We did a piece about him there some eight months back. Got a lot of feedback on it too. Loads."

"I see," said Shane quietly.

❖

When Tommy left, Shane felt restless in himself. He needed a walk, a long walk. He regretted having given the interview. Shutting the front door behind him, he looked up to see that most of the heavy clouds had gone their way. Part of him said to himself that the interview might be a way of introducing himself to the wider community, to the people of Kerry, but another part of him said that he shouldn't have opened his mouth at all. He was way out of his depth, dipping his toe into uncharted seas. As he walked, with each step he began to realize just how little he knew. About anything. Anything that mattered.

A bird chirped. What bird was that? That yellow weed, standing forlorn in the field. What was it? Had it a local name? What should he do? Remain aloof or seek to embrace as much knowledge and infor-mation as was humanly possible? Might his mother's spirit guide him to fields of knowledge which needed to be absorbed—and lived?

"It's the *buachalán buí*, Shane! That yellow thing in the field. It's the ragwort!"

He froze. Who had spoken? His mother? Róisín? May? He knew the voice had told no lie. The Irish word, the *buachalán buí,* and the English word, ragwort. Yes, that's what that weed was. And a useless thing it was, too.

You know more than you think you know, Shane, don't you? he thought. It wasn't just the names of places, people and things that needed to be embraced or re-embraced. Everything had a spirit, too, an all-pervading aura. The music of what happens. Where had that notion come from all of a sudden? Was he too late? Were there always

110

going to be too many gaps? Perhaps if he found a living guide, a friend, a mentor or companion? But who? Nothing he had achieved in life, no case he had solved or failed to solve, no case he had re-opened and studied anew from every conceivable angle, nothing was of any use to him now. The Kerry Detective Agency was nothing but another Kerry joke—without the humour. Was he becoming depressed? Should he see a doctor?

Clouds were coming back. Were they the same clouds of half an hour ago or new clouds? Or old clouds and new clouds coming together? They are floating in my direction, he thought. I'll follow them. Would that I could follow them to the ends of the earth. What did he mean by that? Keep moving and you eventually end up where you started out.

I'm tired, he admitted. Tired of thinking, of feeling, of not feeling. Tired of the way my mind has been used—yes, not how I used my mind, how my mind was used. Tired of the way my mind has become tired. Tired of being tired. What was the sum of his career? 320 people or more found themselves behind bars. So? He had done nothing more than write or revise reports. The records. How many of those 320 would re-offend once released? The irony is that he had edited a report on recidivism. Someone else's problem now. But where was the grace, the goodness, the meaning in his life? What had he done to—and then he remembered. He had helped to find seven children living under a manhole in Slovakia. His little moles, he had called them. Did that really happen? Really? Or was it something he read about? Or just another report? Or a recurring dream?

What will that interview look like in the *Kerryman*? He should have been more honest and said, "Look, Tommy. Most of my childhood memories have been wiped clean. I'm back here in Powl Duv, in my mother's house, but very little is familiar to me. Cherish history. Cherish memory. Cherish detail. Cherish story. You don't have to live in the past, but allow the past to inform the present in some little meaningful way. There's no monument to the poet who lies in Dureen Wood, no plaque, no cairn. Is there? Not a stone or a pebble. Did the Famine do this, did it come between people and their story, their language? My ancestors saw defeat at Kinsale. They saw their chieftains leaving Ireland, never to return. Some of my people settled down, in Powl Duv, in the grip of a severe winter. I am back, among my own. Feeling my way. What is left of my people here? What is left of me? Am I an empty shell?"

"Welcome to Skrahancockgower."

Who or what has spoken? Where am I? thought Shane.

"Cherokee!"

"Meself."

"How did I get here?"

"You must have been whishked along by a fairy wind! Welcome to Skrahan."

"Is that where I am? I don't know how I got here to tell you the truth. I just went out for a walk and kept walking. I'd still be walking if I didn't hear you."

"I do that sometimes meself. I stood on the *fóidín* once, God help us all, and was gone for the besht part of three months."

"What?"

"The *fóidín*. Surely to God you've heard of the *fóidín mearbhaill*?"

"No."

"You're sayin you never—? That's a great wonder so it is."

"There's lots of things I haven't heard of."

"Well, I don't know how a man could go out walkin and not be afeard he might step on the *fóidín*, though I suppose there are millions with no fear of it at all."

I'll let on I know what he's talking about.

"You stepped on it?"

"I did, of course!"

"What is it?"

"If we knew that... we'd know a lot. The Heapies say it's another dimension. They were tellin me about a man—what was his name at all? Was it Davy Lang or somethin like that? David Lang, it's comin back to me now. It was all over the American papers. Vanished he did. In front of his wife. At least I came back to tell the tale. But there's no

112

trace of Lang. Not a smitch or a smidgen. I suppose they've stopped lookin for him by now. If he'd turned his jacket inside out he might have had some chance. That was the way around here. Too late for that now, of course. I often think of him, poor man. I know what it's like. To be away. Anyway, I thought I was only gone maybe an hour or so. Three months away I was."

"You're pulling my leg, Cherokee."

"What would I be wantin to do that for? I had a beard down to my navel, so I had, and further. Go into Tralee and ask for a man called Mick Grimes. His father was the barber. He was a Mick too. It was him that shaved it off. Mick will tell you. His father would still be talkin about it if he were alive. Poor man, died out in the Canaries. His first ever holiday. Back in those days no one took a holiday. They didn't know what it was. They'd call into a neighbour's house for a cup of tea and a story. That was their holiday. Grimes would tell you if he was alive. I told him the whole story from start to finish. It's a pity no one took it down at the time because what happened to me has gone out of my head. I'd say I must be one of the last people alive to have stepped on the *fóidín*, the sod of confusion, so I am. It doesn't happen much any more. It probably doesn't happen at all. I don't know why. There's thousands of things that aren't happenin any more. But I don't let it bother me too much. Why would I? I don't think of changes anymore, changes in people, changes in the world. I'd be more taken in by things that don't change at all and never will. The sun gettin up in the morning. The moon sailin across the sky without a bother. The way a nanny goat would look at you early in the mornin and the dew glistenin on her beard. Not any more. That Belgian fella with his fierce lust for goats, God forgive him!"

And for a minute, Shane imagined Róisín in hot pursuit of the Belgian goat-killer, chasing him all over North Kerry and nabbing him in the end and saving all the goats, each and every one of them, puck goats and nannies and kids.

"Come into the house. You'll have a drop of tay."

"If you're making it."

"I'm always makin it. How are you gettin on since?"

"Fine."

"That's good."

He plugged in a cordless yellow kettle.

"Fancy kettle, that, Cherokee."

"It's fancy all right, so it is. Sit yerself down there. One of the Heapies I was tellin you about, didn't she bring me on a shoppin spree last summer. They're still talkin about it in Tralee, the way the two of us were traipsin around. Sure you wouldn't believe half of the gadgets and paraphernalia I have. I've forgotten what some of them are for. Here take these yokes. I've no use for em."

"Thanks. Are you sure?" asked Shane, looking at a corkscrew and something that was for poaching eggs, at a guess. Strangest thing of all was a set of goggles, to be worn when peeling onions.

"Great excitement up in the village, Shane. I believe May hasn't a bed left!"

"News travels fast."

"You don't mind if I have a smoke?" asked Cherokee.

"You're in your own house. Do as you like."

Cherokee's kitchen was a strange collage of the old and the new, knick-knacks that the hippies had bought for him lying self-consciously next to tattered, torn or stained remnants from other years.

He lit his pipe solemnly, lovingly.

"The water won't be long boilin. She's a fast kettle, so she is. I've no biscuit or bit of cake to offer you."

"I'm fine, thanks."

"The Heapies won't ate anythin with sugar in it. No mate either."

"Vegetarians?"

"Most of em, yes. I asked one of them, Andy, I calls him—Ananda is his name but he likes me callin him Andy, so he does. Says I, Andy, if it's wrong to ate mate, what's a chicken for? And quick as a flash he came back to me and says he, what's a chicken for? What's a human being for, Cherokee? Ah, it was a good answer. I was a long time thinkin about it."

114

Cherokee sighed. Shane wasn't sure was it a sigh of pleasure, contentment, wistfulness or weariness.

"Must be a bit lonesome out here, Cherokee, is it?"

"In Skrahan, is it? I've heard it's more lonesome in big cities, Shane."

Shane wondered at the effortlessness of his own speech, as if words were coming out now without thinking, without measuring their weight.

"You could well be right."

At this, Cherokee looked at Shane, straight in the eye, unblinkingly.

"Don't you know I'm right."

It was a penetrating look which Shane tried to fathom.

"You've lived in cities," said Cherokee, slowly.

"Yes, I have..."

"I can see it."

"Can you?"

What's coming now? What can he see?

"You've seen things you shouldn't have seen."

"Haven't we all? It's an imperfect world." Shane felt tightness in his throat. His palms tingled. Am I sweating?

"And heard things you shouldn't have heard."

"What—what do you mean?"

"Felt things you shouldn't have felt—things no man should have seen, heard or felt. But sure—what of it! It was only all a dream!"

He puffed at his pipe and watched a plume of bluish grey smoke slowly rising and not sure which way it would go.

Shane felt panicky. Had Cherokee seen that his life was a lie with no more risk or danger involved than crossing the road?

The kettle turned itself off. He scalded the pot and put five spoons of tea in it, very carefully. You'd think he was a pharmacist. More like an alchemist, thought Shane.

"You'll have it strong." Shane didn't know was it a question or a declaration. All he knew was that he was enjoying the slow, sure, perfect rhythm of Cherokee's tea ceremony. In a way, that's what it was, an art. Nothing in his movements was amiss. It was all so simple, so natural that Shane was moved, somehow, moved to the depths of his being and

115

grateful, ever so grateful, to have witnessed this everyday yet miraculous activity, so utterly incorrupt, natural, perfect, practised, pure.

"I wonder, I do." he said, nonchalantly.

"What?"

"Somethin you said a while ago. It's an imperfect world. Is it? I was talkin to one of my Heapies about it. A powwow is what he called our little chat. He maintained it's a perfect world."

"Hippies are a bit like that. All you need is love and all that kind of thing."

There was a long pause.

Shane began to worry: had he said the wrong thing? He looked at his shoes. Then he glanced up at Cherokee. The old man reached for two mugs, two old cracked mugs, and poured the hot tea.

"Black. Is that all right?" I've no milk... or sugar, I'm afraid."

"Black is fine."

Cherokee looked into his tea like someone looking into a crystal ball.

"This Heapie says to me, he says..."

Silence. Shane marvelled how comfortable Cherokee was with silence. He seemed to wear it like a cloak.

"Go on."

"Where was I? Oh yes, he says it's a perfect world. It has to be perfect. Otherwise it wouldn't exist. It wouldn't last. It would fall apart. It's a perfect world, he says. Just like a salmon is perfect, he said. Or a rose. What do you make of that?"

Shane looked into the old man's eyes. He saw there a glow, an innocence that he had searched for, longed for, with every fibre of his being. He clutched the chair with both hands, holding back a thimbleful—no more—of hot, foolish tears.

No. How long is it since I have uttered that simple word, No?

Say it. No. No. No!

—Dutch Diaries (destroyed) of Shane O'Neil

Chapter 10

A Whore Pure and Simple

Pain. Anger. Flashing eyes. A disembodied voice. English accent.
Manchester.

"Any questions, boys, about your First Holy Communion? O'Neil!
You look like you might have a question."

"Well—I—just—"

"Stop stammering like a Kerry goat!"

A burst of laughter. Mocking, bleating sounds.

"Silence!"

Silence.

"Yes, O'Neil?"

"Yes, Father. Thank you, Father. No, it's just that—"

"Speak up so that the whole class may hear you."

"Suppose the priest dropped the host, Father."

"Yes?"

"And a little mouse ran out."

Giggles. Suppressed laughter.

"Silence!"

Silence.

"Go on."

How slowly, threateningly, those two words came from the priest's
mouth. Shane felt the blood draining from him.

"And if he swallowed it. Would Holy God be inside the mouse?"

"Up here, you Irish beast, until I beat the demons out of you! Up here!"

Ten lashes on the buttocks.

Another lash.

"And that's for blowing up Nelson's Pillar!"

What's Nelson's Pillar?

His skin is burning.

Another lash.

"There! That's for blowing up Gough."

"I didn't blow up Nelson—or the other fella."

"Don't look at me as though you don't know what I'm talking about, you snivelling Irish brat! You blew up Nelson's Pillar, didn't you?!"

What's a pillar? Who's Nelson? Is there no way out of here? There must be some way out of here. Where's my mother? What happened to my mother? Where am I? Who am I? What am I? What am I doing here?

The doorbell rang. It was the postman, Mick.

"A bit chilly, isn't it? I see you're in the paper!" he said when Shane opened the door. "Nothin like being famous! Here, I'm finished with it. You can have it. There's lots of stuff in it this week. No post for you, I'm afraid. No one loves you! Hold on, there's one. A letter. Who could that be from now?" Shane took the letter—he almost snatched it, and muttered half an apology for his hastiness.

"Thanks," he said, demurely, as Mick went back to his van, engine still running. Off he went. A belch of exhaust.

Shane closed the door and opened the *Kerryman* before sitting down. There was lots about the missing head. Not very coherently written, thought Shane. Deliberately so? The photo of himself showed him with his left hand raised in what could easily have been construed as a fascist salute. His heart sank when he saw the words

DETECTIVE SALUTES SUN GOD

He was made to look like a nincompoop. Or worse. A deranged follower of Mussolini. Poor May didn't fare much better, appearing sadder than she ever did in real life. And look at the words they had put into her mouth:

GIVE ME BACK MY HEAD!

A more amusing piece was devoted to a court case. A certain Johnny Fitzmaurice. Drunk and disorderly. Garda Pat Ryan said the accused called him a whore. What kind of a whore, asked the judge. Garda Ryan was puzzled. You are not from around here, asked the judge. Garda Ryan said he was from Mayo. God help us, retorted the judge. Here in Kerry, he explained, you have lovely hoors, grand hoors, terrible hoors, awful hoors, mighty hoors, desperate hoors, cute hoors, and so on and so forth. Garda Ryan said the accused called him a whore, pure and simple. Fitzmaurice was fined €500.

Shane put down the paper, picked it up and read it again. He wanted to laugh. His chest shook, briefly. But it wasn't a laugh. More of a shudder.

That night he dreamed he was being questioned by that same judge. "You are not from around here? You are not from around here? You are not—"

The dawn chorus awoke him. He got up and went to the window. Bereft of all her children—the stars—a ghost of a moon hung in the sky. He looked across to Dureen Wood, sparkling after a shower of rain. The more he stared the more his gaze became fixed and then seemed to melt until the whole wood shimmered, something hugely, infinitely alive and trembling. Then he saw it. A face. The face of the wood. It was smiling. Every smile that was ever smiled was distilled into that smile. Not a smile of joy or happiness or ecstasy. The smile of self-knowledge, ancient, ever-new, whole and complete; outside of time, outside of space, outside of history, the smile of today and tomorrow and of all time; now far, ever so far in the distance; suddenly near again; and the face was not looking away nor was it looking at itself; its gaze directionless; as the leaves of the wood stirred fretfully, the whole face trembled in silvery silence and the birdsong came to an abrupt end. Shane blinked. The face vanished. It was the wood again where a poet lies buried.

God! God! God!

—Dutch Diaries (destroyed) of Shane O'Neil

Chapter 11

A Letter

S now was falling. His first snow in Powl Duv. As Shane gazed at the swirling flakes, he imagined them to be the souls of dead children revisiting the earth. Some were confused, flying this way and that, as if to say, "Why? Why am I back here again?" Others settled surely and comfortably, glad to be home again. One or two tried to double back, vainly attempting to return to heaven, before being hustled and bustled by all the others down down down to earth.

Snow. What is snow blindness? He had developed a type of snow blindness from reading too many reports. At times, if he looked at the Sphinx directly he wasn't able to see her at all. He could only see her out of the corner of his eye, while looking away. She must have thought there was something seriously amiss. But he couldn't explain. He couldn't stand up and say, "It may appear that I am losing some of my marbles but the reason I am not looking at you is that I see you better this way. I have something akin to snow blindness. I mean no disrespect." Easy to say it all now. Too late. Well, so what. What did it matter? It's all in the past. Gone. Where are the snows of yesteryear?

❖

He had forgotten all about the letter. His first ever letter in Powl Duv. It must be a day of firsts, he thought. How could he not have opened it? It was from a Mr P. J. Moloney, Ballintubber, Co. Kerry.

Dear Sir,

I am Mr P. J. Moloney from Ballintubber and I heard about your set-up only the other day. Good luck to you is all I can say! We need people like yourself here in the Kingdom. There's a lot of conniving and chicanery going on in Kerry and I hope you'll help to put an end to it, or some of it at least. I have a few problems that are troubling me and maybe if you had a crack at the first one I'd send a few more in your way. Would that be fair enough?

I saw my Mrs smiling at herself in the mirror the other day. You never saw the like of it! Smiling at herself. She never does that. Never! I saw her doing it again yesterday morning and when she saw that I saw her you wouldn't believe the scowl on her face. I'd be a bit worried that she might be carrying on, if you know what I mean. Would you be able to take the case? I'll send you a goose for Christmas if you can do it—and two if you catch her *flagrante delicto* I believe the expression is.

I'm enclosing a photo of herself. She's about eight years older now. She goes into Killarney every Wednesday. I'd not be bothering you at all and I'd follow her myself but for my gammy leg. I'd be spotted a mile off.

Yours Truly,

P. J. Moloney, Esquire,

Tooreen, Ballintubber, Co. Kerry

A goose? He might have written the letter with a goose quill as well, such was the wonderful scrawl, very legible, but childlike. Shane read it over a few times and chuckled softly to himself. He liked the Esquire bit. Thank you Mr Moloney, whoever you are. But, hold on, is it real? Could it be a hoax? He looked at the photo of the woman. There was nothing spectacular about her. She was waving, a little shyly. To whom? To P. J. Moloney, Esquire? She appeared to be a perfectly ordinary woman. Honest. Hard working. A decent citizen. Why should he interfere with her life and go sniffing after her like a dog?

He put the photo and the letter back in the envelope and locked it away in a drawer. Taking out a mint, he sat back in a chair, sucked the mint slowly, thoughtfully, closed his eyes and dreamed. What if the letter is a hoax? But who would do such a thing and why? He imagined himself knocking on Mr Moloney's door. A big, burly farmer appears. Shane cannot hear the conversation. It's like a silent movie. He shows him the photo. The farmer doesn't recognize her. It's obviously some kind of an elaborate hoax but Shane has to bear the brunt of it. The farmer is brandishing a blackthorn stick. The film is becoming melodramatic. The wife appears. It is not the woman in the photo. She snatches the photo from Shane's hands, looks at the woman in the photo, and looks at Shane. She looks at her husband. Her eyes are wild.

Whooo! Shane opens his eyes. Had he shouted in his sleep? But he wasn't asleep. It was like seeing the Sphinx; his boss appeared to him, in waking hours and in day-dreaming hours, as a Sphinx, and the doctor said they were going to check on his serotonin levels, whatever serotonin is....

Agitated, he went to the door, opened it fumblingly and took three deep breaths. It had stopped snowing. He could see his breath vanishing in the cold air.

From the PRIVATE DIARY of Shane O'Neil

What was it I saw yesterday? The wood? Myself? A mystic vision? Like a massive yet harmless electric shock. For a moment it seemed I was looking at a galaxy and that I vanished into the galaxy. No longer looking at a galaxy, looking out from within. I was it.

❖

Is that what I was looking for? A life of intensity, with everything happening at its keenest pitch? Or a life of oblivion, nothing happening. Or a life of everything and nothing, happening all at once? Listening to the rain.

Look outside. The first snowdrops, huddled together.

I know what I'll do with Mr Moloney, Esquire. I'll take the case! But do nothing about it. Not a damn thing. Who am I to interfere with their lives? In a month's time I'll drop him a note to say he has nothing to fear. All is well. Whether she is having a fling or not, what he doesn't know isn't going to hurt him.

NB. Barber tomorrow.
Order more turf.
Stock up on mints.
    Irish classes?
    Cooking classes?

I'm going home.

—Dutch Diaries (destroyed) of Shane O'Neil

Chapter 12

A Recession

S hane sat in the barber's chair.
"Are you a son of Mick Grimes?"

"I could be." Shane had heard of certain Kerrymen who were loath to part with any information whatsoever, including the time of day.

"Oh, right. A friend of mine recommended this place. Cherokee Jim. From Skrahan."

"Who?"

"Cherokee Jim."

"What kind of a name is that? Never heard of him. Where's he from, did you say?"

"Skrahan."

"Skrahancockgower or Skrahanaveel?"

"I thought there was only one Skrahan."

"There's plenty Skrahans. Too many of them if you ask me. Will I take much off?"

The door opened. Shane looked in the mirror. A pale youth in a grey hoody sat down on the bench. A heroin addict, thought Shane. The youth picked up a magazine. The cover trumpeted a celebrity wedding.

JANE MARRIES ADAM. EXCLUSIVE PHOTOS.

Shane had no idea under the sun who the bride was, or the bridegroom.

The barber gave a semi-polite cough.

"Parting on the left?"

"Yes."

Shane looked in the mirror and concluded that what he was about to say to the barber wouldn't cause much concern to the sleepy-looking witness behind him on the bench.

"Look," said Shane, "it's—" He pointed to his right ear.

"Hairs in the ears. Would you mind—can you—do you—?"

"Your're havin me on!" says Grimes Junior.

Shane swallowed. He shouldn't have come in and sat down as he did. He should have made enquiries first, over the phone.

"I got it done in Holland once or twice." Shane felt like getting up and leaving but he knew from experience that things would only get worse if he tried to extricate himself now.

"Did they do your nose as well?"

"Actually, come to think of it, they did."

"Look, mate," said Grimes Junior, "I haven't the implements for that kind of operation. Would you not do it yourself or ask the *bean an tí* to do it with a tweezers?"

"Who?"

"The missus."

"Oh yes, *bean an tí*, woman of the house. I've only seen it written. Are you an Irish speaker?"

"No. *Bean an tí* is about all I know."

Shane swallowed again. From the corner of his eye he saw Grimes Junior glancing at Shane's left hand and at the finger where the marriage band should be. Grimes Junior pursed his lips.

I do not like thee, Doctor Fell, the reason why I cannot tell. But this I know, and know full well, I do not like thee Doctor Fell.

"I'll give it a try with the clippers. But I haven't attempted this before, mind, and I'm not responsible for any injuries."

Shane was beginning to regret it already.

"Nose first, or ears?"

"Nose, please."

Dear God, don't let me sneeze.

It was an excruciating experience, during which Shane kept his eyes closed, only opening them when the barber progressed to the more familiar territory of the hair on his head. Both of them were glad when it was all over.

"How much?"

"Fifteen euros. If it weren't for the recession I wouldn't have done the ears and nose at all."

"Here's twenty. Keep the change."

The drug addict looked up as Shane went to the door. His eyes reminded Shane of the eyes of a dog he once saw in Bucharest, one of thousands of stray dogs that Brigit Bardot was trying to save at the time.

As Shane opened the door, he could hear the addict saying, "I'll have the nose job as well."

He closed the door firmly on their sniggering, not looking back.

❖

"It's yourself! Getting the hair done? Just going in myself."

It was Tommy Ashe from the *Kerryman*. Breezy as ever.

Don't let this opportunity slip. Tell him you were unhappy with the photo. Tell him. Now!

"I was unhappy with the photo, Tommy."

"What photo?" He acted as if he were surprised.

"The photo with me and my hand up."

"Wasn't it yourself that asked for it to be that way!"

"I know, but when you used the word 'salute', it made me look like a fascist."

"Listen, I'm sorry about that, Shane. Maybe I can make up for it?"

"How?"

"I'm working on another story. If you'll give us a few comments, we could use a different photo. I took a few without the hand as well."

"What story?"

133

"Europe. Are the Irish Europeans? Like, you were out foreign all your life. You'd be a good man to ask."

Shane thought about this for a moment.

"I'm apolitical, Tommy, I'm afraid."

"Sure that doesn't matter."

Shane offered Tommy a mint.

They both sucked and looked at each other for a few seconds.

"I don't get a great sense of Europe in Ireland to tell you the truth. There seems to be a lot more influence from Britain and America."

"In what way?" He reached for a notebook. "Can I take this down?"

"If you want," said Shane. "What I mean is, music, cinema, clothes, sports, magazines books, TV, the whole shebang, it's all more influenced by Anglo-American values than by European ones. Am I right?"

"You're right. And what's the answer?"

"I don't know. Education? Resistance?"

"Resistance? They love that word in Kerry. Well, not all of them. But a good few do."

"I'm not promoting violence or anything."

"Oh, God no!" Tommy paused. "What are you promoting?"

"Well if there's a tsunami coming, you have to batten down the hatches, don't you? You can't just sit there, waiting to be destroyed. Why isn't there more Irish in the *Kerryman*?"

"Not enough people want to read it, I suppose."

"Why is that?"

"Long story. Must pop in here now and get the thatch done. *Slán!*"

"*Slán!*"

It was the first time someone had said *Slán* to him and his first time to reply. It wasn't exactly a conversation in Irish. Just one word. But it was a start.

Chapter 13

Dances with Octopus

A week went by. Or was it ten days? Or more? Shane couldn't tell. Somehow time plays a different game in Powl Duv. Its own game. Nobody knows the rules. And he thought and thought. Or rather, thoughts came to him, unbidden. He didn't know what to make of his thoughts. Were they his thoughts? Were they thoughts at all? When is a thought not a thought, something half formed, something going back into its own dark source before emerging into the light? And he remembered things. Or tried to remember. There were things to forget as well. So, so much. Part of the brain trying to remember, a part trying to forget, a part going numb, wanting to go numb. But numbness couldn't be the answer, could it? Sometimes, looking at Dureen Wood he managed to dwell in that space between two thoughts and then he felt at home in the universe and in himself. Róisín—could she dwell with him, there? Forever! That space, it seemed infinitesimal, yet vast.

What's easiest? To remember? Forget? He thought of Róisín again. She's not thinking of you, is she? He vowed not to think of her again. Ever. And yet her face appeared. Sometimes, out of nowhere. But did it? He laughed when he thought about this. Did her face appear or did he imagine it? Was he willing it to appear? Her smiles. Frowns. Twinkles. Of course he had only imagined it. Faces just don't decide to appear, do they? I'll appear before Shane now. That's what I'll do. One, two, three! Do you see me, Shane? You have conjured me, I'm here. As what? A genie?

Faces are faces. Just faces. They haven't a mind of their own. They might appear, sure. But only in a manner of speaking. A mirage. An appearance. An optical illusion.

The face of the wood. What was it I saw? The brain playing tricks? A psychedelic flashback to the one and only time he had taken LSD, come back now to haunt him? To explain itself? A mystical experience? While it lasted, it was more real than anything he ever knew in the cold, sober light of day. Watching the face, he knew he was never more alone in all his life and yet strangely unafraid. The face was saying, "I am neither ugly nor beautiful. Neither good nor bad am I. Look at me. I have made myself known to you. Look at me as I am. I am life, glowing shafts of life, a glimpse of all of life, a pulsating smile that is perpetually reborn, over and over again, ever-new, kiss my silvery lips, now and live forever." He didn't. He blinked. And it was over.

I might as well throw in the bloody towel sooner now rather than later, he thought. Close shop. Shop? What a laugh. Missing kittens. Missing heads. Move to Dublin. I'm not made for country life. I was born here, yes, but that was a long time ago. Everybody knows everybody here. They don't know me. I don't know myself. I need anonymity. I'm used to dealing with strangers. Can't function without anonymity. Remember Vienna? You used to walk into that little Greek restaurant off Mariahilferstrasse and order octopus and listen to Zorba the Greek and look at the octopus when it came and not being able to get up and dance because there was no one to dance with except the octopus—not that anyone else was dancing—and one night you did just that, didn't you, you lifted the plate and danced around the place to the rhythm of Zorba, dancing with an octopus, and no one noticed because you had asked for a non-smoking area, *nicht rauchen bitte* and the waiter repeated the phrase incredulously, *nicht rauchen,* as though it might be something shocking and unheard of, and you were totally alone in that section of the restaurant, you danced and you never danced better in all your life—and later, just down the road in the Cafe Ritter, remember, you ordered a coffee and took out a novel and read the whole thing in about four hours and nobody bothered you or asked you were you all right or did you need anything else or, *"Noch einen Wunsch?"* No, no more requests, desires, wishes, hungers, thirsts thank you and the waiters were alert in their own vivid dreams, too busy to notice you, smoking at their leisure, as if the Austro-Hungarian Empire had returned and you were too plebeian-looking to bother with anyway. And the English-language cinema down the road and only four other people in the whole cinema. How do they survive? And *Apfelstrudel* in the café in Schönbrunn and how could you eat it, given the nasty business that had brought you to Vienna in the first place? You learn to swallow. And you forget how to throw up. That's it. That's the game.

What nasty business? Are you insane? Stop fooling around. It was a holiday. Just a holiday. And you walked the streets, gingerly stepping over a few beggars.

Today I heard myself sigh.

How many unheard sighs have I sighed over the years?

—Dutch Diaries (destroyed) of Shane O'Neil

Chapter 14

A Mountain
out of a Molehill

He lifted the phone and put it down again. He had forgotten who he was going to ring or what the call was about. It couldn't have been urgent. He tapped gently on the desk, trying to jog his memory. He lifted the phone again. This time he would make himself remember. He put the phone to his ear. There was a click. A definite click. What was that, he thought? Am I being bugged? Who would want to bug me? Europol? Do they listen in on former employees? He had heard of such cases. Not many. But a few. He put the phone down. He picked it up again. Or the sergeant? Could Róisín be involved in this? Perish the thought.

"I'll make a complaint," he said to himself. "Or report a fault." He found the number to ring.

"Hello? Ron here. It's Ranjit really but please call me Ron. How can I help you, Sir?"

"Hello. Yes. My name is O'Neil, Shane O'Neil."

"Irish? I love the Irish. Everyone in this call centre loves you!"

Shane was taken aback. To be told by a stranger that he was loved was a new experience.

"You do? Ron, excuse me. Where exactly are you?"

"New Delhi, Sir."

"New Delhi? India?"

"Exactly Mr O'Neil. Now how may I help you? I love the Irish. You know, it was your great poet Mr Yeats who helped our great poet, Rabindranath Tagore, to get the Nobel Prize?"

"Really? No, I didn't know that."

"I have lots of facts about Ireland. Longest river Shannon. Correct, Sir?"

"Correct."

"Capital city, Dublin."

"Correct."

"Highest mountain? Yes, I used to know this." Ranjit or Ron began to hum. He didn't know the answer. The little hum became an em–em–em and Shane sat there as if listening to a mantra that eventually would dissolve all the thoughts that were swimming around in his brain.

"No, it is eluding me."

Shane had heard of outsourcing but this was his first experience of it. Was there nobody in Tralee or Dublin who wanted to take his call?

"Carrauntoohil, Ron. Not far from here as it happens."

"You joking! That's the name. Now you say it, I recognize it. Very difficult name for me. Never heard it said out loud before. Can you say again, please?"

Shane said it again.

"You say it very nicely. I like this name. What does it mean?"

Shane didn't have a notion. Without knowing exactly why, he invented a meaning.

"Goddess whose head is high in the mist."

A five-second silence followed and then a deep sigh.

"Beautiful. How high is it, Shane? You don't mind me calling you Shane, Shane?"

"No, it's OK. I mean, it's fine."

"So?"

"So? The reason I'm ringing is—"

"No, first, Shane, please, how high is goddess mountain, if you don't mind."

Shane didn't mind. The voice on the other end of the line was lively, friendly, animated.

"I think it's just a little over a thousand metres, Ron."

"Goodness me! A thousand metres. And this you are calling a mountain? It's a molehill. I think you are making mountain out of molehill. Have you ever been to India, Shane?"

"Afraid not, Ron."

"Ah, Shane. You must come to India. I will show you mountains. The Western Ghats. The Himalayas." He began to cough.

"It is raining now in your country, Shane?"

"It's been misting on and off for a few hours."

"Very dry in New Delhi , Shane, very dry. All this month. As dry as flour. I dream of walking in the mist. Standing in the mist. Standing at the foot of your goddess." The coughing started again.

"Far-away hills are green, they say. Are you all right, Ron? Ron?"

The coughing continued.

"Must be hard on your voice, Ron. Your job. All the talking. You should keep some mints handy." The coughing stopped. When he spoke again, it was in anxious, hushed tones.

"It's OK, Shane. False cough. Supervisor looking at me."

"Oh, I know all about it, Ron. Supervisors. Huh! Does she look like a Sphinx?"

"Thank you for your call, Mr O'Neil. The matter will be investigated first thing tomorrow morning. Good-bye."

Ron hung up. Shane felt like a falling leaf, falling silently into a dead silence.

Chapter 15

A Dear Little Plant

In a dream Shane saw the whole population of Powl Duv, most of whom he had not seen before, and all of them, himself included, were parading through the village. And all sorts of people were greeting him and they knew his name. How you doin Shane? How's she cuttin, boy? It was St Patrick's Day. Cherokee Jim, Thady, May, Mick the Posht. And for a second, he thought he saw his mother in the crowd. Is that you? Mammy, is that you? Mammy, will you comb my hair? She vanished.

Little Bella was there, the white kitten, with her one black ear. She was alive! And Dureen Flyer, the greyhound, he too paraded, in all his glory. Hopping along the road, flying a few yards, then hopping again as if trying to keep up, was a robin.

Shane could hear himself singing an anthem along with everyone else:

There's a dear little plant that grows in our isle,
'Twas St Patrick himself, sure, that set it;
And the sun of his labour with pleasure did smile,
And the dew from his eye often wet it.
It shines through the bog, through the brake, and the mireland,
And they call it the dear little Shamrock of Ireland...

And the more he thought of the words, the more ridiculous they sounded. Tears of mirth trickled down his cheeks. Ridiculous or not, he had remembered them, and the tune, exactly as he must have learned it as a boy. Buried deep in his mind all those years abroad, those trite words and sentiments.

Why does the mind dream up and remember certain things while a range of other memories and sensations remain beyond recall? He got out of bed and washed his face. Could he see his mother's face in his own? His father's? He began to shave. Who had taught him how to shave? Had he taught himself?

He nicked his left cheek. A little trickle of blood flowed down to the edge of his mouth. Whose blood is this? How old is it? Does it die with me?

Chapter 16

Will I Tell You a Story?

It was just the three of them (and the barman) in O'Dea's, Cherokee, Shane and the Infant Jesus of Prague. The TV had been switched off. Thady was polishing glasses, slowly, methodically. First he gave them a spurt of steam from the coffee machine, then he polished and polished.

Cherokee had been ensconced for some time before Shane joined him.

Why was there a little statue beside his tumbler of whiskey?

"Stories. That's all they had before radio and television," mused Cherokee.

"And have you any yourself?" Shane asked, hardly able to keep his eyes off the statue.

Cherokee looked at Shane. He wasn't expecting the question.

"Oh, I had them all right. Once upon a time. Plenty of them. It's too many stories I had. But no one to tell them to. I told a story to one of the Heapies once. It must have been too long. It was about the Battle of Ventry if you ever heard of it."

"No."

"No?"

"Afraid not." No point in racking his brains. Shane was sure he'd never heard of it.

"No matter. It was an awful long time ago. He fell asleep. The Heapy. It must have been too long for him. There's six hours in it if it's told with all the proper trimmings. Will I tell you a short one?"

"Do," said Shane, without thinking, not knowing what was about to come.

Cherokee looked around him.

"Sure, I might as well. Don't fall asleep on me now."

He giggled a bit and shoved back his peaked cap almost to his hairline.

"Haven't told this one now in fifty-odd years, would you believe it. Or more. I hope it'll all come back to me. I've the bones of it anyways." He looked away into the distance.

"I'm sure it will come back to you," said Shane, encouragingly. Cherokee didn't hear him. He was already in the realm of tales. It was as if the old man's breathing had stopped. A spurt of steam from the coffee machine and he started to breathe again. He looked at Shane and Shane saw in his eyes that he had returned from that other realm with his story intact.

"An awful thing it is to murder a story. Or a song. Right, so, are we ready? This is about Daniel O'Connell, the Liberator, you know. You must have heard of him."

"I did," said Shane. If the truth be told, his knowledge of Irish history had huge gaps in it.

"Who hasn't heard of him? The greatest man to come out of Kerry. Though I met a man once who had no time for him at all. O'Connell, he said, the man who had more Irish than the Pope has Latin and he refusin to speak a word of it. It's the O'Connell Monument and not Nelson's Pillar they should have blown up, says he. But I don't know. The same man admitted he had some affection for Dan. I was in Dublin once and I saw the seagulls shittin on the O'Connell Monument. 'Twould never happen down here. Well anyway, that's another matter entirely. Most people around here worshipped O'Connell and the holy ground he walked on. A great man for takin a bet was Daniel. One day anyway didn't this smart fella come up to him and says he to Daniel, Daniel says he, with all your eloquence, says he, and all your mighty words, says he, do you think now, says he, do you think you could get one half of a crowd laughin and the other half cryin, says he, all at the

148

same time. Daniel looked at him. You little pup, he says to himself, is it tryin to outwit me you are? Sure hadn't Daniel outwitted all the wigs and the peers over in England? Didn't they say he outwitted the Devil himself? Would this be some class of a wager, says Dan. It would, truly, says the other, I'll wager you fifty pound. Now fifty pound was a lot of money in those days, Shane. I don't know what it would be in euros today but I'd say we'd have eatin and drinkin in it for a couple of years, the two of us. Anyway, Daniel took the bet. Never turned down a bet in his life. Never. Right so, what did he do? I'll tell you what he did. He hired a hall for himself inside in Tralee. I'll show you the spot some day, so I will, though it's seldom I venture as far as Tralee these days. But anyways. What did he do? He put a kind of a platform or a stage or somethin in the middle of the hall, do you see? Well, he got talkin anyway and once he got started, don't you know, he wasn't goin to finish at all and he had the crowd in front of him cryin and moanin and he tellin em about all the woes and injustices and misfortunes and sorrows that had visited poor Ireland. And plenty of sorrows there were to relate too, that's for sure. But wasn't the crowd behind him in stitches. Groanin with laughter they were, men, women, and young wans."

"Why is that?" asked Shane.

"Sure couldn't they see what the crowd in front wasn't able to see at all—Daniel O'Connell and no arse to his trousers!"

Shane laughed. He put his hand to his mouth but the laughter came out in spurts. He was laughing, not so much at the story, but at the triumphant look in Cherokee's eye. He had told a story and told it well.

"Very good, Cherokee. I love it."

And when he saw the delighted twinkling in Cherokee's eyes he laughed all the more.

"Mind you, Shane, only Daniel could have thought of it—and got away with it. Ah, 'twas cheeky of him though, wasn't it? I do be thinkin of things like that meself but carryin them out, that's another can of worms entirely."

"Have you another one? Go on! Please!" said Shane, almost beggingly. He hadn't laughed so much in years.

"Will I have another?" Cherokee looked at the statue.

"No, I said have you another. Another story."

"Oh..."

"But you'll have another all the same?"

Cherokee looked at the statue. So did Shane.

"I suppose it will be all right..."

"What's with the statue?"

"He keeps an eye on my drinkin. How many was that? Another will be the fifth. Right. One more so, Shane. Good man yerself."

Thady brought the drinks and patted the statue on its cracked, miniature head.

"Yes, lots of wonders I see in Ireland," he said. "Lots and lots of wonders. Cherokee being spinning some tales, eh? I too spin tales. Am writing a book. Mr Smith in Tralee give me advance. One hundred euros. *A Pole in Powl Duv* it is called. Is good title? Mr Smith says it has a ring to it. It would be easier to write about a Pole in Tralee—because here, nothing happening. But *A Pole in Tralee* has no ring to it. This is what Mr Smith says. Must have a ring, he says."

"Good man," said Cherokee. "Have you much of it written?"

"Just the title," said Thady a little despondently. "You like anything else, Mr Cherokee?"

"Maybe I'll have a coffee."

"Maybe means yes, no? Latte, cappuccino, espresso?"

"I don't speak Polish, Thady."

"That was Italian, Mr Cherokee."

"Two americanos," said Shane.

"Coming up!"

Shane and Cherokee clinked glasses, watched closely by the Infant Jesus. Then Cherokee looked away again to the Realm of Tales.

"No man ever got the better of Daniel. Ever. And that's the truth. But a woman did..."

"Go on..."

"And Daniel after savin her from being transported to Van Diemen's Land—that's where they'd send you if you were a thief."

"And was she a thief?"

"She was that, poor thing. An O'Riordan she was. None of her crowd left now. Not a soul. All in America. Butte, Montana. An ould nanny goat it was she shtole, one that belonged to the herds around Skrahan-cockgower. I suppose she wouldn't have shtolen it at all if she wasn't in the need of it, the craythur. Milk. She got into debt anyway and had to sell the ould nanny. That left her with nothin at all but a pig and the pig was no good. Sick. A sick pig is no good. She became more desperate by the day, you see, and the pig gettin sicker, so what did she do, didn't she shteal the nanny goat back. She did, faith. And they caught her. Poor woman, she explained her case to Daniel. Will you defend me, says she? Daniel never lost a case but he didn't particularly like the look of this one. So he thought and he thought and..."

Cherokee put a finger in his ear and took out a small bit of wax, twirled it and flicked it away.

"I've got it! says Dan. He'd thought of a way out, you see. The woman was over the moon. You'll defend me so, says she. I will, says Daniel. But, says he, how will you pay me, says he. I have a pig, says she. Daniel was mad for the pork. A grand pig, says she. A brave grand pig. A healthy pig she is, too. A fat brave grand healthy pig. She's yours, Counsellor, every bit of her if you can get me off. OK, says Dan. Here's what you must do. And he explained it all to the woman, over and over again. They'll arrest you and stand you in the dock and they'll ask you your name and they'll ask you this and they'll ask you that and they'll ask you t'other and all sorts of things and did you steal the goat and did you steal it back a second time and all that and more. They'll confuse you and confound you with all sorts of things and you won't know is it Latin or English or Irish you're listenin to. Sufferin Jesus, says the poor Riordan woman. Now you are to do as I say, says Dan, or you'll be transported, woman, do you hear me? I hear every word you say, Counsellor, says she. Now, says he, there's only one answer you'll give them. Whatever the question. Only the one. And what's that, says she? Would you ate a scallion, says Dan. I would, says she. No, says Dan, I wasn't askin you would you ate a scallion. I'm tellin you what to

151

tell them. Would you ate a scallion? Say it! Would you ate a scallion, says she. Again, says Dan. Would you ate a scallion, says she. Good, says Dan. Say nothin more. I have you Dan, says she. She didn't know what it was at all but if Dan said to say it, sure it must be a magical formula or somethin, that's the way she was thinkin. She put all her faith in him. Like many another. Sure what else did she have? Well, she was dragged out and her name was called and she stood in the dock and the case began. What is your name? asked the clerk of the court. Gibbons was his name. His people are still in Tralee. And dacent people they are too. Would you ate a scallion, says she? Gibbons stared at her and his two watery grey eyes began to bulge in his head and the left side of his face started to twitch a bit. The poor woman just looked at him. The judge's bushy grey eyebrows began to go up and down in a terrible way. Answer the question, says the judge, or it will be the ship to Van Diemen's Land. She looks at the judge and says, Would you ate a scallion? Do you hear what I said, thundered the judge and his face blackened and reddened and reddened and blackened. Would you ate a scallion, says she again. What is it the confounded woman is sayin, says the judge to Gibbons. Sure Gibbons didn't have a clue. What are you sayin at all, says Gibbons. Would you ate a scallion, says she again. Take her away, says the judge. That woman is crazed in her intellectuals. Case dismissed. She got off free. Daniel was waitin for her outside the court. He was very partial to pork, was Daniel, and he loved a bit of cracklin so he did. He'd keep the cracklin till the end of the meal, crunchin it slowly and washing it down with a sup of port that he had kept from a shipwreck off the coast of Ivereagh. What was the name of the ship? *The Lady* somethin. It's gone out of my head, Shane."

Shane looked at him, bewildered. Had the story ended? Cherokee took a sip of whiskey, savoured it a while before swallowing it and licking his lips with great satisfaction.

"As I said, Dan was outside the courthouse in Tralee, and out comes the woman herself and she lookin as pleased as the Queen of Sheba.

Now my decent woman, says Dan, let us go and collect this fine fat pig of yours.

"Would you ate a scallion, says she to Dan and that's all he ever got out of her. Would you ate a scallion! True as God! He was stumped! You could say 'twas his own cleverness that brought him down."

Shane laughed out loud. "Brilliant, Cherokee, brilliant."

"Dan was a brilliant man—but he was up agin a brilliant woman."

Thady arrived with the two americanos.

"You never married yourself, Cherokee?"

"Never did, Shane." There was a hint of a sigh. "Too much of a wanderin eye in my youth I had. Never fixed the eye on the right girl. But what girl would want to settle down in Skrahancockgower, tell me that and tell me no more. It do be a lonesome enough place when the curlew calls of an autumn evenin. I mean, lonesome for a woman. Meself, I don't mind it at all and from what I've heard about Chicago, I'm better off where I am."

They sipped their coffee in silence. Cherokee tipped the remainder of the whiskey into the coffee.

"He didn't see that, did he?" he said, glancing at the statue and winking at Shane. Then he put the statue away in his coat pocket and got up, his feet unsteady.

"I'm OK, I'm OK."

Shane looked worried.

"Let me walk back with you."

"All the way wesht to Skrahan, is it? You will not."

"I will so. Let's go."

Outside O'Dea's, a broken umbrella sat against the wall, something spent, defeated, useless, exhausted. He hadn't seen it earlier. How long had it been there?

"Are you sure yer up to it, Shane?"

"Why wouldn't I?" He was conscious that he had answered a question with another. I'm settling fast into Kerry ways, he thought. "No bother, Cherokee. Skrahan here we come! Skrahancockgower."

"You say it lovely so you do!"

"Cock is the goat, right?"

"No, cock is the shit."

"Cock is the shit?" Shane smothered a giggle. "Gower must be the goat then."

"Now you have it in a nutshell."

Shane felt cheerful and knew exactly why. Not only was the local accent easier on his ears than he thought it might be, he found himself doing something useful for a change, accompanying old Cherokee home. All those years of pen pushing. For what? He had achieved nothing. Endless bureaucracy. Reports. He used to have nightmares about them. In these nightmares he was a slave, an Egyptian slave. His bosses pharaohs. Building pyramids, he and a thousand other slaves, pyramids of reports. One morning his chief supervisor came along and when he looked at her she was the Sphinx. You're OK, the psychologist said. I think she's a bit of a Sphinx too.

"Did you ever hear of the Sphinx, Cherokee?"

"The what?" and the old man cocked his ear.

"The Sphinx?"

"Is it a washin-up liquid? I don't watch much television to tell the truth."

"Ah, you're better off, Cherokee. Do you have a television?"

"No, I don't. I'd say it musht be an awful thing to be watchin it on your own and no one beside you to say what an awful thing it was you were watchin."

"You never had anyone? A partner?"

"Well, no. Not really. I was fond of someone once to tell you the truth but she went with another. He turned out to be no good. He left her. She deserved better, poor May."

"May Kelly?"

"Say no more, Shane, like a good man."

There was a silence between them, nothing but their footsteps on the road to Skrahan. The moon came out. Cherokee bent down and picked up something, rolling it curiously between index finger and thumb.

"Badger droppins," he said. "They're back."

From the PRIVATE DIARY of Shane O'Neil

I now know what to say in Irish if someone sneezes: *Dia linn!* (God be with us.)

If there's a second sneeze, *Dia linn is Muire!* (God and Mary be with us.) A third sneeze and you add *Pádraig* (Patrick). A fourth and you add *Bríd* (Brigid) to the litany. A fifth and it's the turn of *Colm Cille* (Columba) to come to the rescue. After that you simply say to the sneezer, *"Capall bán fút!"* "A white horse under you!" I have failed to discover the significance of this phrase. Might it be meaningless? I have practised the litany many times now and I think I have it to a tee. But I haven't had the chance to use it yet. I wish somebody would sneeze...

May Kelly dropped me in the *Kerryman* with the feature on Europe. True to his word, Tommy had used a photo which showed me to be a fairly sensible-looking fellow:

TSUNAMI WARNING

Shane O'Neil, the Powl Duv-based detective, formerly of Europol claims we are not letting enough European culture into the country. We should resist the rubbish that comes from the Anglosphere, he maintains stoutly. Resistance is the only way if we're not going to drown in a tsunami of Anglo-American flotsam and jetsam.

Local Fine Gael TD Pascal Brosnihan criticized O'Neil. "These are inflammatory remarks and do nothing to help tourism in Kerry. A former policeman should know better."

I shouldn't have stuck my nose into it at all. Let them sort it out among themselves. I've been reading Douglas Hyde, first President of Ireland. Even back then, in 1892, he was talking about the necessity of de-anglicizing Ireland. It wasn't just the language; his generation looked to other cultural markers, sports and the like. Why not revive a whole cultural package, to include clothes? Clothes make the man. The Scots have no problem sporting the kilt. The Indian is not ashamed of the dhoti. Why did the Irish reject traditional wear? Hyde had a mantra, "Down with Trousers!" I like the sound of it. Will order an Irish kilt.

Chapter 17

The Poet Who Never Was

"**T**his is it. This is Skrahan. And there's my humble abode. You'll
come in, Shane, and have a cup of tea—or somethin stronger?"
Nothing indicated that they were in Skrahan. Not a sign anywhere. Why
did he expect a sign? How does Powl Duv become Skrahan all of a
sudden? Were there other unsigned townlands between Powl Duv and
Skrahan that they had passed through just now, unbeknownst to Shane?

"Are you sure, Cherokee? It's not too late?"

"What's late or what's early? Sure it's only Greenwich Mean Time—
somethin else that was once ours before they stole it from us! Or so I'm
told. Well, they're welcome to it. Come in now, come in. I haven't done
a bit of spring cleanin in years but I don't think you're the class of man
to mind a bit of dust."

"There's no harm in it."

"I'll stir up the fire, so," said Cherokee, "and I'll put down the kettle.
Here, have a read of that while you're waitin." He had taken down what
seemed like a scroll from the dresser but what Cherokee had handed to
Shane was a yellowing copy of the *Kerryman*. An old edition, going
back eleven years. On the front page was a story: 'The Poet Who Never
Was'.

"What's all this?"

"An ould story. An ould mystery if you like. It's never been solved.
You might solve it someday, you being in that line of business. Would
you read it out loud for me?"

"I will of course."

Shane sat down by the table, spread the page out slowly, as though handling a Gaelic manuscript that he had just dug up in a bog, and began to read: "'There was anger and disbelief among the people of Powl Duv when Professor Donncha Ó Briain of the Irish Department, University College, Cork, delivered a lecture in that city to a small audience in which he declared that the Poet of Powl Duv never existed.'"

"Did you ever hear the like of it!" exclaimed Cherokee, still in shock, eleven years after the event.

Shane looked up quickly and then continued to read: "'The poet, says Ó Briain, is simply a composite, that is to say, the fragments of his poetry that still exist in parts of Kerry are actually the work of various hands. Indeed, the Professor claims—pouring more petrol on the fire— that there is dialectical, sub-dialectical and stylistic evidence to suggest that extant lines of poetry—much of it doggerel—and popularly attributed to the Poet of Powl Duv were, in effect, stitched together by itinerant poets around the time of the Famine; if we untangle this unholy mess, we will find that the original lines, in all their purity, were the work of none other than the legendary poet Máire Bhuí Ní Laoghaire who was born in Túirín na nÉan, Co. Cork, in or around the year 1774. Computer-driven stylometric analysis backs up our hunch.'"

"This is amazing, Cherokee."

"'Tis. Scandalous. There's more on page 8!"

Shane turned to page 8. "'Reaction has been furious in the local area. Headmaster of the Gaelscoil in Tralee, Ruairí Ó Dúill, had this to say: "First they say he didn't exist at all. Or if he did, whatever he was or was not he wasn't a Kerryman. In fact, he wasn't even a man. But a Cork woman. When and where is it all going to end? We can't sit down and allow Kerry poets to be poached in this way! It's time to make a stand. If we look back at Kerry history, a lot of our poets had a very hard time of it. Piaras Feiritéar was hanged by the neck in 1653. Aogán Ó Rathaile suffered the indignities of poverty—having to eat periwinkles and the like. Eoghan Rua Ó Súilleabháin, as if he didn't have enough hardship being knocked about in the British Navy, didn't he get a knock on the head when he came home and not even the charms of a red-headed beauty and she pulling up her skirts for him could revive him. I could go on. The list is endless. And now they're saying that the Poet of Powl Duv never existed at all. A figment! It's the final ignominy. We won't stand for it. As for doggerel. I've seen some of Professor Ó Briain's poetry and it's not a patch on our man. Not a patch! He had a poem there in *Comhar* a couple of years back, and talk about doggerel, a dog would have made a better job of it. I'm a graduate of UCC myself but I'm returning their piece of parchment to them—by registered post, in case they claim they never got it. And I see they're getting their computers to do their work for them now. Computer-driven stylometric analysis, God help us. The poet of Dureen saw it coming so he did. He saw the day when the donkey would no longer bring churns of milk to the creamery and machines would come along and take the place of poetry. This is what he said:

> 'Ní thriallfaidh an t-asal go mall ar an gcréimire,
> Meaisíní gan mheidhir againn in ionad na héigse...'"

"God, Shane, you said the Irish there like a native."

"I've been practising, listening to a few CDs, Cherokee."

"Have you, faith? Of course, the teacher had to admit later on that the lines you just quoted there weren't by our man at all."

"They weren't?"

"Not a bit of it. People were inventin verses all the time and sayin they were the work of the Poet of Dureen but was it out of mischief or somethin? I don't know. Some kind of divilment. Or a craze. Poetry was pourin out of people, people that didn't think they had a line in them. I heard that some of it ended up in Chicago. Why they brought it to Chicago with them I don't know. Anyway, read on there, Shane, like a good man!"

"Right, Cherokee: 'Local Fianna Fáil councillor Patricia Devine was having none of it either. "This is not the first time UCC has poked its nose into Kerry affairs. I've been saying it for years and I'll say it again.

It's time Kerry had its own university. If Cork has a university and Limerick has a university and Galway has a university—and isn't Dublin bristling with universities—isn't it high time we had one of our own here in Kerry? Let's have it, Kerry University—Ollscoil Chiarraí—to look into our own culture and to do our own research. Isn't it a well-known fact that Cork poets and Cork professors are jumping over themselves coming down here to Kerry all the time to brush up on the Gaelic? If they don't show a bit more respect for our Kerry poets, maybe we shouldn't let them cross the border at all!'" What happened in the end, Cherokee?"

"Yerra, it was only a storm in a teacup, Shane. Speakin of which, I've no sugar or milk. Would you mind drinkin it black? I've a drop of the craythur to add to it if you'd like."

"A wee drop so..."

Cherokee took a noggin of Power's whiskey from a drawer, opened it, put it to his nose and poured some into Shane's cup and then into his own.

"It's a pity you weren't here the summer of two year ago. I could have offered you a duck egg. I hired a few ducks and a drake the time the Heapies came over. They love a duck egg. Except for Andy. He's a vegetablearian and won't even touch an egg. Won't even eat a cheese sandwich. There's rennet in cheese, he says. It comes out of a calf's belly. *Sláinte!*"

They clinked their cups.

"What's under the water but never gets wet, Shane?"

"God, you have me there."

"An egg inside in a duck!"

"God, Cherokee, I don't know where you get them from—so, tell me... what happened about the poet? Did they find out if he existed or not?"

"He went mad in the end."

"The professor?"

"No, Shane, the poet. No one could make head or tall of his verses anymore. I suppose they'd let the language slip by then and turned to the English, don't you know. Or it's the way they didn't want to know

160

about it anymore. It was the poor man's language. Poor man, it's said he started talkin to the badgers. It's the badgers that have his poetry today. That's what they say anyway. Me friend Andy says it could be true. You're not a vegetablearian yourself, Shane, are you?"

"No, Cherokee. I'd eat anything."

"Very gentle soul that Andy fella. He do always be sayin God is in everythin. Even in yer man over there."

Shane looked over. A mouse had appeared in the corner, its little grey whiskers twitching.

He looks a bit hungry, thought Shane. I wonder would he eat a mint?

"I'll be making a move so, Cherokee."

"Here, before you go. Take this."

"What is it?"

"Guess."

Whatever it was, it was wrapped in old newspaper.

"Heavy," said Shane.

"It's the head. You'll bring it back safely now, won't you?"

From the PRIVATE DIARY of Shane O'Neil

As I carried the head back to Powl Duv, my first thought was—what
if Sergeant O'Brien drives by? I'd be in a right pickle then, trying to
explain things, wouldn't I?

So, another mystery solved. Cherokee pinched the head. I would
never have suspected him. Had a soft spot for May Kelly. Hoped her B
& B would fill up with all sorts of people, experts from the Museum up
in Dublin, tabloid hacks, photographers and the devil knows who else.
But the few that turned up were locals and didn't stay long. May was
left with a load of rashers and eggs and black pudding and tomatoes.
I'm just back from her place now. She fed me like I was Napoleon's
army.

She doesn't know who borrowed the head—or why—or who returned
it. Not a clue.

❖

I haven't thought of Europol in a long time. Suddenly, out of the blue,
a batch of reports came to mind, analytical reports on new legislation
in the Romanian Parliament. Everything had to be examined and reports
had to be written. New legislation nearly always had implications for
Europol's work. I can remember some of the bullet points.

Prevention and Fight against Social Marginalization
Prevention and Sanctioning of Money Laundering
    Witness Protection
Prevention and Fight against Organized Crime
Certain Measures to Ensure the Protection of Victims of Crime
Protection and Promotion of the Rights of the Child
International Judicial Cooperation in Criminal Matters
National Social Welfare System

The realization that I would never have to write or read another report brought such a choking feeling to my throat that the only way to release this flood of emotion was to yodel. And yodel I did for a good twenty minutes. I felt good afterwards.

Chapter 18

A Goose

It was Mick the Posht. Shane recognized his rap on the door. "Guess what I have for you?" He was holding something heavy behind his back. Shane wasn't in a guessing mood.

"I don't know, Mick. What is it?"

"A goose!"

Shane looked at the unplucked bird.

"Got one meself, too, so I did. In case she might be writin letters to young bucks, I've orders to report the matter to him at once. Did you ever hear the likes? Sure he's stone mad that fella. As cracked as five hundred Orangemen on parade he is. Here you go now," and he handed Shane the goose. It had a label on it. 'Here's the goose.' Sorry it's not two.

"I see the head's back."

"It is."

"You weren't workin on the case, were you?"

"No, I wasn't, Mick."

"Right so. It came back by itself I suppose. Like the last time. I've somethin else for you here." He handed Shane a parcel.

"I'll be off now. Take care."

"Good luck!"

It was a big goose. Too big for Shane's oven. And anyway, he didn't know how to cook a goose. Time to repay May Kelly's kindness.

He knocked softly on the door. As he waited, he noticed a snail climbing the wall of the house, its head slightly tilted to the left.

"Keep going!" whispered Shane. "You'll get there yet, wherever it is you're going."

He looked again at the goose. Sympathy arose in him. Was it killed on my account, he thought.

The door opened. Shane realized he must have cut a droll figure, standing there with a downy goose in his arms.

"Glory be to God!" exclaimed May.

"If you cook it, May, we could sit down and eat it together. What do you think?"

"Good-lookin goose, Shane. Looks like a Moloney goose from Ballintubber, would I be right?"

Not for the first time, Shane was left speechless.

❖

Back home, he opened the parcel. His kilt had arrived. A saffron kilt. He stroked it, over and over again.

"Beautiful!" he whispered.

Chapter 19

Incident in Dureen Wood

One night Shane awoke to the sound of a piercing scream. Was it a dream? He looked at the small clock on the sideboard. It was after two in the morning. A scream! Definitely, a scream. Again! He rose quickly, lit the lamp that gave off a faint orange glow and put on his dressing gown. He hurried to the window and opened it. The scream had come from Dureen Wood. What was it? He listened. He could hear his heart thumping, like something inside him trying to get out.

The night was impenetrable. He could see nothing. Not a glimmer. Again he heard a scream of pain and terror. It cut through him. It was most definitely a cry of distress, a female cry. A woman was being attacked. But who? Who would be in Dureen Wood at this unearthly hour? What should he do? He decided not to waste any more time thinking about it. This was a police matter. He would have to ring the gardaí in Tralee.

"What?" said the voice on the other end of the line. "Are you sure? And you are? Right, Mr O'Neil. Do nothing, do you hear? Nothing. Stay in your house, please. Do you hear me? Good. Dureen Wood you say? We'll get a car there immediately. Your call has been recorded."

Shane put down the phone and breathed a deep sigh. He put his hand in his dressing gown pocket and found a mint. He looked at it, placed it thoughtfully in his mouth and chewed on it for a while. But it didn't bring about the calm and assurance which he normally associated with this activity; instead he felt an unease accompanied by sudden pangs of hunger. The house was cold. He closed the window. Was that another scream in the distance? He shuddered and went to the kitchen, put on the light and moped about. Do nothing, do you hear?

He paced the floor for a good ten minutes. He looked to see what provisions he had in the house. Very little. Onions. He could make onion soup. But first he would light a fire. This he did and waited for the blaze. Would anybody see the smoke coming from the chimney? Who else was awake at this ungodly hour? Who else had heard the scream? A spider emerged from a crevice.

I remember you! You still around? Find yourself a wife yet?

He went up stairs. The kilt was folded on a chair. He decided to try it on. It looked good. Really good. He mightn't wear it in public, but around the house... why not? He put on a crisp, white shirt and began to talk to himself in the mirror, in Irish:

"*Dia dhuit!*"

"*Dia is Muire dhuit.*"

"*Bhfuil tú go maith?*"

"*Tá me go maith, buíochas le Dia. Conas tá tú fein?*"

"*Go maith.*"

He had managed it effortlessly: Hello. Hello. Are you well? I am well, thank God. How are you? Fine.

It wasn't earth-shattering. Pedestrian stuff really. He peered into the mirror, as if expecting that this his very first conversation in Irish, albeit with himself, had transmogrified him in some manner or left an indefinable aura behind. Nothing.

He thought he heard the scream again. He went down to the kitchen and washed his hands. Anything, anything to keep his mind off Dureen Wood and not to think of the unspeakable acts that were going on there. He switched the radio on and sat down. Anything to drown out those pitiful cries. What was he listening to? Gluck's opera, *Orpheus and Eurydice*. No, not that, please! It would be so beautiful at any other hour but not now, no, please, not now!

And Orpheus sang:

> Enough, enough, my friends!
> Your grief increases my own!

Scatter purple flowers,
place garlands on her tomb,
and leave me!
I would remain alone
among these dark and mournful shades
with the pitiless company of my misfortunes!

The music had frozen him to the chair. He could not endure it but endure it he must.

Soon it would be dawn, he thought.

How clear the sky! How bright the sun!
How new and serene is this light!
What sweet, enchanting harmony
do the song of the birds,
the purling of the streams,
the murmur of the breezes
make together!
This is the abode
of the blessed heroes.
Here everything breathes peace and contentment,
but not for me.

Finally, he extricated himself from the chair. Orpheus had to be stopped or one of them was about to crack.

Her sweet voice,
her loving glances, her tender smile,
are my only, my blissful Elysium!
But where can she be?
Let me ask this happy crowd
which comes to meet me.
Where is Eurydice?

Shane silenced the radio. It had taken all his effort to do so. He paced the floor, stopped, breathed in and out for a few minutes before eventually recovering a degree of serenity. He remembered that he was hungry. Onion soup, the only thing.

He spotted the goggles that Cherokee had given him. They were still in their packaging. Why not try them? Goggles for peeling onions. Who would have thought? They fitted rather well and Shane commenced to chop a few onions, carefully, precisely, as if a life depended on it.

Now to put some oil in a pot and—the doorbell rang. Shane threw some chopped onions in the pot and hastened to the door. He would remember this night for a long time to come, or rather he would try not to remember it.

Sergeant O'Brien, accompanied by Róisín, were looking at him, an expression of horror and disbelief on both faces. It was then he realized he was still wearing the goggles. He removed them quickly and spluttered an apology.

The sergeant was trying to bore a hole in Shane's forehead with his eyes.

"Sorry, is it you are?" said the sergeant. "You're sorry, is it? What are ye sorry for, O'Neil? WHAT?" A strange growl. Suppressed anger of a dormant volcano coming to life after a thousand years. Shane was confused. It was unreal. This was a play. The sergeant had spoken his lines but Shane had somehow missed his cue.

It was only when Róisín looked down, at his pale knees, that he remembered he was wearing the kilt.

"Shit!"

"WHAT?" said the sergeant.

"What?" answered Shane.

"WHAT, is it? Is it WHAT?" bellowed the sergeant.

He wasn't making much sense to Shane. He was just a fuming mass of flesh, belching meaningless words. A cock began to crow.

Mental hygiene. Imagine him as something else. Quick! A circus clown! No. It's not working. Something else. Statue of a Buddha. Yes, that's it. It's working. He is a statue of a Buddha. He cannot hurt you or harm you in any way. Now, ask the Buddha about the woman. How is—

"The woman. How is the—?" And Shane could see the dreaded yang sanpaku in the Buddha-Sergeant's eyes.

"WHAT?" said the Buddha-Sergeant.

Róisín wore an expression that said I wish he'd stop saying that.

"Woman? Woman, is it?" said the Buddha-Sergeant, in a tone that suggested he was trying to explain something to a complete moron.

"Yes!" said Shane, emphatically, but respectfully, seeing he was addressing Lord Buddha. "How is the poor woman?"

Róisín closed her eyes. The cock crew again. Startled, she opened them. Such lovely eyes, thought Shane.

"Woman? Woman? Is it how you've never in your life heard the sound of matin badgers, you complete and utter boshtoon you!"

Shane looked at Róisín, looked at the Buddha-Sergeant, looked at Róisín again and pointed a finger to his own eye, nodding, indicating the sanpaku state of the Buddha-Sergeant.

"What is this, WHAT? Are you tryin to tell me somethin? What's he pokin his eye for, Róisin?"

Róisín tried to calm him down.

"'Tis all right. The man meant well, Sergeant. He meant well."

There was a burning smell.

"Come on, Róisín, a stór. Let's get back to Tralee. We'll deal with this later on. Wastin police time is a serious offence, Mr O'Neil. Or is it Mrs O'Neil?"

He glanced contemptuously at Shane's bare knees.

"Very serious indeed. We'll be back."

Shane could hear a sizzling sound from the kitchen.

"Shit! My onions!" he groaned and disappeared.

From the PRIVATE DIARY of Shane O'Neil

In a book of quotations, I found this:

Beidh lá geal gréine go fóill in Éirinn.

"There will be a bright sunny day yet in Ireland."
The Great O'Neill.

I have adopted it as my prayer.

Chapter 20

Jenny Apfelbaum

On her way to Shannon Airport by taxi, Jenny Apfelbaum suddenly said, "Pull over." The driver looked in the mirror to check what was wrong. Nothing, it would seem. Americans tended to be fussy, in his experience. She had probably spotted a spider or something or other minding its own business on the back seat.

"Let me hear that thing!"

The driver turned up the sound.

Radio Kerry was reporting on the Incident at Dureen Wood, as the story had been billed. She shoved her spectacles down her nose and began to take notes, furiously, page after page of notes. The driver pretended to ignore her but glanced in the mirror every now and then, amazed at the speed with which she transcribed what was being said.

A local wildlife expert was being interviewed:

"Badgers usually mate in February but in Dureen Wood they seem to mate whenever they feel like it."

"Whenever they feel like it?"

"Yes. They are at it all the time."

"I see. And could you tell our listeners, did you ever mistake that sound... you know, when they're at it—did you ever mistake it for a human voice?"

"Me? Personally, no. I know a little bit about badgers. But it doesn't surprise me at all that Mr O'Neil made that mistake. Not in the least."

"Do you know where this Powl Duv place is?" said Jenny, looking at her watch.

"I do," said the driver. "We'd have to turn back. About fifteen miles, I'd say."

"Could you get me there?"

"Sure."

"If I hop out and take a photo, can we still make my three o'clock flight?"

"If I put the boot down."

"Do it," she snapped.

Jenny has been assigned to write a photo-essay on Kerry, the usual tourist hotspots, Connor Pass, Slea Head, the Skelligs, Killarney. Her gut instinct told her that the Powl Duv story might be more valuable. She had enough notes taken for a short, three-hundred word piece. A filler. She could polish it while waiting for her flight and send it to her agent from the VIP lounge. She might be lucky with this piece. It had an unusual mix of ingredients. All she needed now was a photo.

"Let me know when we get to the wood. I need some shots of the wood as well."

"I will, Miss. Very strange story that. Strangest I heard in a long time. Will you be writin about it?"

"I am writing about it."

"I won't disturb you so."

"Do you know this O'Neil fellow?"

"I'd know him to see."

Jenny thought about a title. "Badgers Fool Kerry Detective". No. "Kerry Sleuth Badgered". No. "Kerry Gumshoe comes Unstuck". No. Keep trying.

❖

Shane had taken an early lunch and decided he needed a brisk stroll. Morning showers had brought out a few young snails and Shane bent down to lift one out of his path. That was when Jenny Apfelbaum took a photo that went around the world with the caption

He Hasn't a Clue!

From the PRIVATE DIARY of Shane O'Neil

It's been two months now since Miss Apfelbaum's snippet was syndicated. To be ridiculed by the local media is one thing. But the incident in Dureen Wood went all around the world, America, Australia, Europe, Asia, Africa. You can be sure the staff in Raamweg 47 were choking over their coffee-break biscuits. One mistake, one little slip up is enough to land you in the soup. Whatever prospects I might once have had with Róisín are trodden deeply in the mire. Kerry people never forget anything. This is going to haunt me for the rest of my days. Jenny Apfelbaum. Why did you do this?

In fairness, there's a good side to it. The friends I've made! Unbelievable! I cannot put faces to their names but letters came pouring in. From everywhere. Mick the Post was flabbergasted. Never seen anything like it! There were ignorant, abusive letters, too, of course. How do people find time to sit down and write a letter to a complete stranger, calling him jackass, cretin, fathead, birdbrain, dingbat, galoot, dummkopf, pinhead, putz, goofball? Most letters were favourable, however. This is my favourite one and I write it out here, word for word.

> Esteemed Mr O'Neil,
>
> Fraternal greetings from Mauritius. Our Society meets once a month to look at all stories, big and small, that make the news. Your story came to our attention and as Honorary Correspondence Secretary I have been asked to communicate to you our very good wishes and tender blessings.
>
> We have nothing to say about the fictitious woman in the woods except to say, if it is any comfort to you, that the world is something of a fiction anyway, in the view of the jñānis (sages).
>
> We would very much like to comment on the photograph, however. Ostensibly it appears to be a detective looking for, or, perhaps, examining a clue, does it not? We know it to be

otherwise, esteemed Sir. We detect in it your heartfelt care for the lowliest things that crawl upon this earth.

The world's media are, sadly, saturated with distressing images of himsā (violence). The touching photograph of you and the baby snail was ahimsā (non-violence) to the very core. If you are ever in Mauritius, drop in for a refreshing cup of tea. It will be served, I assure you, on a silver platter.

OM SHANTI SHANTI SHANTI!
I am, Sir, most respectfully yours truly,

Dr Kali Prasad Bhattacharya
Honorary Correspondence Secretary
The Theosophical Society of Mauritius
Indian Ocean

Chapter 21

The Heapies are Coming

Time rolled by. It was summer again. Shane began to take long walks, usually in the direction of Skrahan. One day Cherokee met him on the road.

"I've a letter here from Andy. They're comin, Shane. They're comin at last! The Heapies are comin!"

Shane grinned from ear to ear.

"That's great news."

"And look! Have a look at this!" Cherokee was clearly delighted by something and Shane couldn't wait to hear his good news, whatever it was.

"Look!" Cherokee was holding a piece of paper in his hand.

"What is it?" asked Shane. Something about Cherokee's demeanour had filled Shane with a boyish excitement, something he hadn't felt since he was given the Beano Annual on his fifth birthday.

"It's the Lord's Prayer, Shane. In Cherokee!"

"You're joking me!"

"As sure as the sun is beamin straight down on the two of us, Shane. The Lord's Prayer. In Cherokee. Can you believe it? Come on, we'll say it together, will we?"

"I haven't said a prayer in years, Cherokee."

"No more than meself. But look!" and he handed Shane the sheet. "Look, it's gas! It gives an explanation and all. Our Father, heaven dweller *O-gi-do-da*. I suppose *da* is the Father? What ya think?"

"God, I don't know, Cherokee. Good guess. It could well be."

"Here," and he tugged Shane by the sleeve, "pull over here out of the sun and we'll say it together."

"OK so." It was the least Shane could do to please his friend. His best friend. His only true friend in the world.

Cherokee took his cap off. Silence, except for chirping insects in the meadow. Slowly, like schoolchildren learning to read, they stumbled through the text, not knowing anything about pronunciation, rhythm or emphasis. Some words made them laugh. And if they messed up a line, they said it again until eventually they reached *Amen*:

ᎣᎩᏙᏓ ᎦᎸᎳᏗ ᎮᎯ,

Ogidoda galvladi hehi,

Our Father, heaven dweller,

ᎦᎸᏉᏗᏳ ᎨᏎᏍᏗ ᏕᏣᏙᏫ.

Galvquodiyu gesesdi detsadovi.

My loving will be Thy name.

ᏣᎪᏫᏳᎯ ᎨᏒ ᏫᎦᎾᏄᎪᎢ,

Tsagvwiyuhi gesv wigananugoi,

Your Lordship let it make its appearance,

Ꭰ ᎢᎦ ᎣᎿᎥᎾᎵ ᏱᏓᏄᏗᏍᎩᎢ.

Ani elohi winigalisda hadanvdisgvi.

Here upon earth let happen what you think,

ᏁᏍᎦᏯ ᎦᏄᎸᏗ ᏥᏂᎦᎵᏍᏗᎭ.

Nasgiya ganulvdi tsinigalisdiha.

The same as in heaven is done.

ᏂᏓᏙᏓᏢᏒ ᎣᎦᎵᏍᏓᏭᏗ ᏏᎩᏏ ᎪᎯ ᎢᎦ.

Nidadodatlusv ogalisdayvdi sgivsi gohi iga.

Daily our food give to us this day.

ᏗᎨᏍᎩᏫᏒᎢᏉᏃ ᏕᏍᎩᏚᎬᎢ,

Digesgivsiquono desgidugvi,

Forgive us our debts,

ⵔⵙyⵧ ⱨⱠꙅ‬ꚗⱰⱡ‬ kⱨꙅy,

> *Nasgiya tsidigayotsineho tsotsidugi,*

> the same as we forgive our debtors,

Dɗ LⵧⱭ ꙨꙆⱯꝶⱬⱭ꙲ ⱧR ⵔⱭꙨyⵧⱭꙆꙨ꙲ⵔWⵔ·y,

> *Ale tlasdi udagoliyediyi gesv widisgiyatinvstanvgi,*

> And do not temptation being lead us into,

ⵔꙨyꬶLⱹⵧꙆ꙲ⵧⱭꝆꙨyh ꙨꙆ ⱧRT.

> *Sgiyudalesgesdiquosgini uyo gesvi*

> Deliver us from evil existing.

GⱱꝆⱬⱬZ GEꙨGⱭ ⱧRT,

> *Tsatseligayeno tsaguwiyuhi gesvi,*

> For thine your Lordship is,

Dɗ GꝆhyⱭⱭ ⱧRT,

> *Ale tsalinigidiyi gesvi,*

> And the power is,

Dɗ RGⱰⱴⱭG ⱧR hⱭⱭⱭT.

> *Ale etsalvquodiyu gesv nigohilvi.*

> And the glory is forever.

RⵔꙆⵔ·.

> *Emenv.*

> Amen.

Cherokee whistled, a little whistle of pure wonder.

"We did it, Shane."

"We did."

"There's not a lot of people in Kerry who can say the Our Father in Cherokee."

"Be sure of it."

Cherokee rubbed his hands with glee.

"Ah, they'll be here soon, the Heapies. They will, to be sure. I can feel it in my waters. Can you feel it, Shane?"

"Well, maybe, yes..."

What exactly is meant by feeling something in one's waters, thought Shane. He closed his eyes, expecting to feel some trickling sensation. Nothing. Nothing out of the ordinary.

Cherokee put his cap on again, took out his pipe and examined it. He was like an archaeologist, thought Shane, making a careful study of an artefact. After some humming and hawing, Cherokee decided it needed a bit of cleaning and pulled a pipe cleaner from the top pocket of his jacket.

"They'll be wantin all sorts of news and stories, and entertainment, Shane. We'll be worn out as sure as God."

"We could have a barbeque."

"A barbeque?"

"Yeah, a big party. Out in the open. Eating and drinking and singing and dancing and telling all sorts of stories."

"That would be mighty! Mighty so it would. I could tell em stories about Daniel O'Connell. Sure, haven't I tons of em."

"You have. I know you have. And great stories they are too."

"Faith and you haven't heard the half of them yet."

"And I can tell them all about the *meithiagán*."

"You have me there, I'm afraid," said Cherokee, pausing, pipe cleaner poised in mid air.

"Little red insect that appears on the first of June."

"Is that a fact?"

"It is."

"And today wouldn't be the first of June would it?"

"It would."

"Isn't that a wonder. Well, we'll have to keep an eye out for him so. Little red fella you said? It's a great big name for a wee little fella. That's for sure. Anyway, it's goin to be great, Shane, I'm tellin you now. We'll be dancin around in a circle. And we'll get Thady to do the barbecue. Andy will be wantin a vegetablearian sausage. I tried it once meself, the vegetablearianism."

"Did you? How did it go?"

Shane knew in his heart that he treasured these conversations with Cherokee more than anything else on earth. He could never anticipate the drift: a story, some arcane wisdom, some folly and much as he loved talking to Cherokee, he loved the pauses as well, the silences between them, as though they shared some deep secret the nature of which he would never know.

"I only lasted four days. Was ready to chew me own leg off."

"God above!"

"I don't know how Andy does it at all. It's a mystery."

Shane looked up at the sky. It was thronged with beings, some human, others not, all waiting for an official invitation to the barbeque.

"Thady, we'll need him to be sure. He's a decent cook, most of the time. Now, who else? May Kelly, of course. Where would we be without May?"

"A queen she was! She was a queen, Shane, when she was younger. A walkin talkin queen. You mightn't think it, but she was. Hmmm... you'll be invitin, what's her name, Róisín, I suppose?"

Shane smirked. "Goes without saying. She mightn't come though. She might be busy. If she can't come we'll invite Bridgit Bardot. She loves stray dogs."

"She sounds nice. The sergeant has a thing about stray dogs. They drive him mad. Will you be invitin the sergeant, Shane?"

Are you being a bit mischievous, Cherokee, you old rogue?

"We can't invite everyone, Cherokee. Can we? Anyway, he doesn't like me very much. I don't know why. It must be because of the business with the badgers."

"God that story spread far and wide, didn't it? I declare to God! Well anyway, it's not about the badger business at all, Shane. It's because you're an O'Neil."

"And what's wrong with that?"

"Isn't he an O'Brien!"

"And what if he is?"

"Look!" And Cherokee started describing a route on his hand with the pipe cleaner. "Watch me now. When ye were comin down from the North that time, you know, for the Kinsale business."

"Yes, what about it?"

"Ah well, nothin. Nothin serious. Ye did a wee bit of a detour, that's all. Look, do you see here, where I'm pointin to? Ye stopped around about here and ye took a swipe at the O'Briens."

"We did?"

"Oh ho, ye can be sure of it. Split a few heads."

"Why did we do that? I'm very sorry to hear it."

"Don't be a bit sorry. They were all at it then. Sure that O'Brien eejit would only put a damper on the party anyway."

"He would too, I suppose. What about P. J. Moloney?"

"Goosey, is it? We'll have to invite his missus as well. And they can be keepin an eye on each other and drivin each other mad!"

"Wouldn't it be great if Fritz could come?"

"'Twould. Who's he again now?"

Cherokee was having difficulty keeping track of all the guests.

"A yodeller."

"What in the name of God is that?"

"Someone who does yodelling."

"I know that. But what is it?"

"You've never heard of yodelling?"

"Not that I know of. Whatever it is, there was never much call for it in Skrahancockgower."

"It's a bit like this..."

And Shane began to yodel. There was a commotion in the bushes and a blackbird flew off.

Cherokee's mouth opened in wonder and Shane looked up and allowed a passing cloud to bring him sailing to the Swiss Alps. He had never yodelled like this before, out in the open air. He felt like a boy who had just learned how to whistle. When he finished, Cherokee looked at him quizzically.

"Does it hurt?"

184

"Hurt?"

"Well, Shane, they way you were twistin your mouth an all, I thought maybe—come here to me, do people do that for a livin?"

"Some do, yes."

"Do they really? Wonders never cease. I'd say it's hard work all the same. You're sweatin!"

Shane wiped away a bead of sweat that had run down his forehead on to his nose.

"I was thinking one night to myself, Cherokee, as I was yodelling along with Fritz on the radio, I was thinking if only Fritz could teach Sergeant O'Brien how to yodel, it might take some of the bile out of him."

"He's a sour man. No truer word. Did I ever tell you about the snuff box?"

A snuff box? Now, how did we get around to that?

"I was all alone in the pub. Just meself and the statue and me thoughts and Thady. Poor ould Thady hadn't much English at the time so there was no point sayin anythin to him. And he couldn't understand me very well either. His English came out of a book, you see. It wasn't real English at all. Well, not the way we speak it around here. Anyway, there I was mindin me own business when O'Brien marches in and the young wan with him."

"Róisín?"

"Yes. What have you got there, says he. That's the Infant Jesus of Prague, says I. Leave him out of it, says he. That other thing. What's that? Snuffbox, says I. What's in it? says he. Sausages, says I. WHAT? says he. He has an awful way of sayin WHAT. Snuff, says I. Snuff? Isn't that the same as tobacco, says he. Is it legal to have snuff in a public bar? I never heard tell it wasn't, says I. Test it and see is it snuff at all that's in it, says he to the young wan. Her eyes started to bulge, Shane. She couldn't believe her two ears. Test it, he says. How, says she. How do you think, says he. Shove it up your nose. Hand over the box, says he to me. Thady didn't know what was goin on. He got into a bit of a panic. I saw him knockin back a couple of hefty swigs of

185

spirits. Vodka. That's what the Poles drink, isn't it? Good luck to them. Anyway, where was I? Oh, yes, yer wan takes a bit of the snuff anyway and sure maybe it was her first time ever but whether it was or not the next thing you know isn't she sneezin all over the sergeant. I nearly piddled with the fit of giggles so I did. I'm confiscatin this, he says and he took the box. I'm goin to check it out with the Office of Tobacco Control. Yerra, what is it, it's only a bit of snuff, says I. Never saw it since, Shane. It was a lovely wee box. An uncle of mine had it before me and he got it from another uncle, out in Chicago. It saw many a good wake, or so me uncle told me, many a good wake so it did, here and abroad, that same little box, wherever it is now."

"That's terrible. Here, have a mint."

"I won't bother. I think I'll light the pipe."

"Do! Do! Let me tell you, Cherokee, I'm really lookin forward to this barbeque."

"So am I. We'll invite everyone, everyone now, do you hear?!"

"Everyone! Your man, the Belgian goat-killer. What about him?"

"Gezelle, is it? Wherever he is, the rogue. He'll never set foot in Kerry again, I assure you. Not if he knows what's good for him. Sure, one of the goats he killed, wasn't it elected to be King at the Puck Fair in Killorglin. Oh, there was *mile murdar* about it, I can tell you."

Shane chewed a mint, confidently. He racked his brains. Glancing now and again at Cherokee, the old man looked on admiringly. Anyone would think that Shane was about to discover the Law of Gravity or something of similar weight.

"We'll invite... hmmm, let me see now. Who else do we know? Johnny Fitzmaurice. He was fined €500 for being drunk and disorderly. It was in the paper. But he's a reformed character by now, I'd say. Hey, speaking of the paper. There's Tommy Ashe. Do you know Tommy?"

"Is he the man that took yer photo?" Cherokee looked at Shane quizzingly.

"You saw the photo?"

Cherokee nodded.

"With the hand?"

Cherokee nodded again.

"You said nothing about it."

"I didn't."

"And you saw the other one. Picking up the snail. The one that went around the world?"

"I did. Isn't it framed inside in Moriarty's pub."

"Is it?" Shane didn't know whether to feel shame or a certain pride.

Cherokee looked away and sucked air through his mouth; someone trying to forget something. Shane hadn't seen him do that before. He began to blabber and ticked off names on his hand:

"And all those lovely people who wrote to me. Esteemed Sir! A man in Mauritius called me esteemed Sir! All those lovely people. And Fernando and—and poor old Takiguchi and Mick Grimes, even, and Jenny Apfelbaum and Ron and—Donn!"

"Hould your horses there, Shane. Who are—? Who's Donn? And who's this Ron fella?"

"Donn is a fairy prince. And Ron, Ron is an Indian friend. His real name is Ranjit."

"Indian? Like meself. Does he like dancin?"

"He does. Loves it. I haven't danced myself since I danced with an octopus. In Vienna."

"You danced with an octopus?"

"I did, Cherokee, I did."

"You're a remarkable man, Shane O'Neil. Did any one ever tell you that?"

"No, Cherokee. You're the first. I wonder should we invite that fella, Brian Smith? You know, The Cat's Pyjamas. Maybe not." Cherokee was distracted by something and Shane spoke, his eyes raised, as though talking to God. "I'd love to invite the starvelings, the hungry ones I saw on the road, heading for the coast. Did they ever make it?"

A jacksnipe called. Or was it a curlew? A stranger among men and among birds, Shane couldn't rightly tell. He listened. It was a mournful sound. Shane snapped himself out of it suddenly, startling Cherokee.

"Cherokee! I might wear my kilt! And play the tin whistle."

"A kilt is it? Sure that would be grand! Do. Why not. The Heapies won't mind a bit. Sure won't some of em be as naked as the day they were born, God willin, if this weather houlds up."

Cherokee rubbed his chin.

"I'll have to take the scarecrow out of the shed. The Heapies love the old scarecrow so they do. I've no use for him meself, not since I sold the good field. Have you ever seen me scarecrow? Sergeant O'Brien says he looks a bit like meself. I suppose I was supposed to take offence at that but I didn't. Yerra, not at all, boy. Not a bit of it. Why would I? It was a compliment really. That's the way I look on it. The Heapies love lookin at the scarecrow. They sit down and look at him for an hour or more, whatever it is they see in him. A kind of a staring match. My fella always wins! They gave him a name and all so they did. What was it agin? Edgar. Edgar Allan Poe. I suppose he must be the only scarecrow in Ireland with a name. What do you think?"

"Maybe in the whole world."

"In the whole world? Wouldn't that be amazin! Edgar Allan Poe. I says, why do ye call him that and they say because he's po-faced. I don't know what they do be sayin half of the time, when they're speakin American, but it's lovely to be listenin to them all the same. Anyway, I can't think of anyone else to invite, can you? Mick McCarthy, I suppose. It's good to be well in with the postmen. They say he's going to be made redundant. Not enough letters. Now, is there anyone else? Hould on!" He sucked at his pipe. It had gone out. He took it from his mouth, looked at it and snapped his fingers.

"I suppose, Shane, I suppose we'll have to invite Duán while we're at it, hah?"

"We will of course. But not the head!"

They nearly fell over themselves laughing:

"No, no, God above, not the head," chuckled Cherokee, wheezing, almost out of breath. "He can leave his ould head behind him so he can."

ALSO AVAILABLE FROM EVERTYPE

NOVELS

Elisabeth: Excerpts from the diary of a Mennonite girl in the Gran Chaco
(Peter P. Klassen, tr. Jack Thiessen 2016)

She: A History of Adventure (H. Rider Haggard 2016)

Pride and Prejudice (Jane Austen 2015)

Strange Case of Dr Jekyll and Mr Hyde
(Robert Louis Stevenson, illus. Mathew Staunton 2014)

Three Men in a Boat (To Say Nothing of the Dog) (Jerome K. Jerome 2013)

The Hound of the Baskervilles (Arthur Conan Doyle 2012)

The Carrollian Tales of Inspector Spectre (Byron W. Sewell 2011)

Treasure Island (Robert Louis Stevenson 2010)

Nautilus (Craig Weatherhill 2009)

Twenty Thousand Leagues Under the Seas (Jules Verne, tr. F. P. Walter 2009)

Through the Looking-Glass and What Alice Found There (Lewis Carroll 2009)

Alice's Adventures in Wonderland (2nd edition, Lewis Carroll 2015)

STORIES

Kwaidan: Stories and Studies of Strange Things (Lafcadio Hearn 2015)

Nosy Neighbours: Stories in Mennonite Low German and English
(Jack Thiessen 2015)

Neighbours: Stories in Mennonite Low German and English
(Jack Thiessen 2014)

The Partisan and other Stories (Gabriel Rosenstock,
tr. Mícheál Ó hAodha & Gabriel Rosenstock 2014)

The Book of Poison (Panu Petteri Höglund & S. Albert Kivinen,
tr. Colin Parmer & Tino Warinowski 2014)

The Burning Woman and other stories (Frank Roger 2012)

www.ingramcontent.com/pod-product-compliance
Lightning Source LLC
Chambersburg PA
CBHW020329260626
47156CB00004B/1445